The Four Corners of the House

ILLINOIS SHORT FICTION

THE FOUR CORNERS
OF THE HOUSE

Stories by
Abraham Rothberg

UNIVERSITY OF ILLINOIS PRESS

Urbana   Chicago   London

Publication of this work was supported in part by a grant from the Illinois Arts Council, a state agency.

"The Red Dress," *Epoch* (Fall 1954).
"The Animal Trainer," *University of Kansas City Review* (Autumn 1954).
"The Pearl Fishers," *Pacific Spectator* (Winter 1955).
"Roman Portrait," *New Voices II* (1955)
"The Dürer Hands," *Transatlantic Review,* No. 18 (Winter 1965).
"Pluto Is the Furthest Planet," *The Yale Review* (Winter 1965); reprinted in *Best American Short Stories* (1966).
"The Sand Dunes," *Southwest Review* (Spring 1968).
"Polonaise," *The Massachusetts Review* (Winter 1974); reprinted in *Best American Short Stories* (1975).

Library of Congress Cataloging in Publication Data

Rothberg, Abraham.
    The four corners of the house.

    (Illinois short fiction)
    Contents: The red dress—The animal trainer—The pearl fishers—[etc.]
    I. Title.   II. Series.
PS3568.0857F6   1982   813' .54   81-10464
ISBN O-252-00922-3 (cloth)   AACR2
ISBN O-252-00926-6 (paper)

For Bommo

And, behold, there came a great wind
from the wilderness and smote
the four corners of the house,
and it fell upon the young men,
and they are dead; and I only
am escaped alone to tell thee.

—Job 1:19

Contents

The Red Dress

When Anna came out of the hospital, the sunshine was still fitful
and undecided, but the wind had changed direction and was blowing
the city smoke and the quiet-looking, detached clouds over the East
River toward Queens. Waiting for Jessica—since Jessica had quit
social work and become a housewife, she was never on time for an
appointment—Anna smoked a cigarette and thought about the red
dress. She had seen it in the window of one of the very expensive little shops on Fifty-seventh Street and from the moment she had seen
it on the tailor's dummy, Anna knew that she wanted it and that it
was impossible for her to have it. She had gone in nevertheless,
noting the saleswoman's carefully calculated stare at her cheap
tweed coat and her navy blue knitted cloche, enduring it because she
wanted to know how much the dress cost. The saleswoman, a tightly
corseted woman in discreet gray, with a high upswept mass of tinted
black hair, had taken out a mate to the one in the window and Anna,
hat and coat off, had held the dress, hanger and all, against her
while she looked at herself in the full-length mirror. She saw the
length of red silk fall beautifully away from her body and felt the
softness of the material between her fingers as she held it to her
waist. The saleswoman hadn't bothered to offer to let her try it on,
and before Anna could ask, the woman carefully told her the price.
"One hundred and thirty-five dollars," she said, smiling almost
with relish. "Reduced from a hundred and fifty-eight fifty." Anna
had put her coat and hat back on, murmuring a subdued thank you
and, not taking her eyes from the dress, had then gone out onto

Fifty-seventh Street hating the coarse feel of her tweed coat and the sight of the well-dressed mink-clad women on the street.

That had been three weeks ago and she had gone by that store window on some pretext or other every single working day since. The dress had been there until yesterday, when in its place was a gold taffeta evening gown. Because it had replaced the red silk, Anna hated it fervently. She had mentioned the red silk to Jessica and Jessica suggested that they try the sample house where Carol Van Wyck, a mutual friend, got all of her clothing.

"Are you still mooning about that dress?" Jessica was standing in front of her, grinning her wide-mouthed friendly smile so that the crow's feet showed around her eyes.

Anna laughed and stubbed her cigarette out underfoot. As they fell into stride and walked crosstown, she said, "So help me, I feel like a case myself. I never was like this about any dress. It's almost like a fixation."

"You'll get over it," Jessie said. "I feel like that at least once a week, but Vince usually talks me out of it. Can't afford it, he says."

"How is Vince?" Anna said, asking after Jessica's husband.

"Still finding that there are hundreds of promising young lawyers in New York, and none of them making a decent living," Jessica laughed. "How about you? Handling a big case load?"

"About sixty active," Anna said, "but that's par for the course right now."

"No wonder you got a fix on that dress. You're overworked."

"Sure, but who isn't?"

"Anything special?"

"The usual, and the most painful, the kind you can't do anything about. Refugee whose lovemaking was done in D.P. camps without privacy so long that he can't make love any more. His wife wants a child, among other things. Old lady who can't swallow and doesn't know why. She thinks she's got cancer of the throat, but there's no trace of it. The psychiatrist says her children have been planning to send her to an old folks' home and she doesn't want to go. She wants to die, so she can't swallow food. Oh, you know what it's like, with stuff buried so deep they don't really know what's happening to them or what they're looking for." As she said it, Anna realized that her desire for the red dress was a search too, for something entombed inside her that she couldn't or perhaps wouldn't see.

"You been going out much lately?" Jessica asked after a while, just a shade too gently, Anna thought. Everyone was very careful now since she had turned twenty-five and was still single, even Jessica, as if she were now officially doomed to lovelessness.

"No, not much," Anna said.

Jessica nodded, clucking sympathetically, and they walked on in silence, a silence Anna was grateful for. Jessica always knew when to talk, always had, even when they'd been in social work school together. Jessica sensed when she had something on her mind, even if it was only a red dress. Or was it only a red dress?

Mae Rumage's place was on the fifth floor of a big, dark office building in the West Seventies. The elevator operator said, "Miz Rumage's place is the last one down on the left," and they walked through the dim corridors, feeling the strange quiet of an office building after hours. "Five thirty-six" had small rubbed-out black letters with the name, *Mae Rumage,* and beneath, in letters equally worn, the single word, *Samples.* Jessica knocked, first quietly and then loudly until the frosted glass pane in the door shook like chattering teeth, but no one answered.

"Guess she must have forgotten," Anna said, almost grateful that the place was closed. She shouldn't feel that way about a dress and if they found no one and went away, maybe the feeling would go away too.

"Carol called her for an appointment at two this afternoon. How can anyone forget that quickly?" Jessica asked, irritated.

"You looking for Mae?" The voice was behind them, hollow in the narrow corridor, and they whirled, startled.

Anna nodded almost automatically, seeing a hairy man in an undershirt, a razor in his hand, his face half-lathered, and looking completely alien in the impersonal, office-like corridor. In the yellow light, Anna saw that a leather belt around his waist ended in a holster that held a revolver. Anna stared at the gun, so inharmonious against the pale skin, the dark hair, and the washed-out undershirt, almost believing that Jessica's whispered "He's got a gun!" was her own voice echoing in her head. The man suddenly noticed that they were staring. "Don't worry, girls, I've got a license for it. I'm a private detective. See!" He pointed to the gilt lettering on the glass of his door. It read: *William Frey, Executive Surveys.* "That's my office. Come on in. I'll call Mae for you."

"No," Jessica said, "it's all right. We'll come back some other time." She took Anna's arm and began to pull her toward the elevator.

"She lives just down the block," Frey said, "won't be any bother. She probably just went home for a . . . bite. Probably forgot you were coming. She's a little forgetful, about some things."

Reluctantly they followed him into his office, and sat in the straight-backed chairs while he called. "Mae?" he shouted into the phone, "you gotta coupla customers here. Nice-looking girls too. Been waiting for you fer forty minutes. Maybe more. Said you had an appointment with 'em. Sure. Sure. But get over here fast." He hung up.

"You shouldn't have told her we were waiting so long," Jessica said. "She'll be angry. Besides, we only just got here."

"Won't bother Mae. But you better buy something. She'll cuss you up and down if you don't." He went into an adjoining bathroom, left the door open, and went on shaving. Anna could see the gun nestled at his waist as he raised his arms in shaving, looking like some darkly exotic corsage pinned there. She took out a cigarette, offered one to Jessica automatically, forgetting that Jessica didn't smoke, and then, with the cigarette in her mouth, discovered that she didn't have a match.

"Wanna match?" His face still lathered, Frey watched her rummaging through her purse.

She nodded. He walked into a room that led from the office and in a moment called from the other room. "Come on in here and I'll give you a light."

Anna looked at Jessica, and Jessica whispered, "Just yell and I'll come running." She grinned mischievously. "If you don't, I'll know you're enjoying yourself."

Anna walked into a room that had a large studio couch in the corner, turned down for sleeping, and next to it a large blond mahogany buffet. "You work late, Mr. Frey?" Anna asked.

"Who, me? Naw, nine to five for me." Frey picked some matches from the buffet, struck a light for her and lit her cigarette. "Drink?" he suggested in a hoarse whisper, leaning toward her, the match still burning between his fingers. "Scotch, rye. . . ."

" . . . no, thanks," Anna said, finding her voice, and discovering it had fallen to a hoarse, conspiratorial whisper like Frey's.

"How about the fights? I'm going tonight and we could make a time of it?" he said, looking at her hopefully. He waited another moment and then, shaking the match out, he dropped it, threw the book of matches back on the buffet, and went out ahead of her.

When he had finished shaving, Frey put on a white shirt he took from a desk drawer, and a dark tie, readjusted his holster, and turned away from them to tuck his shirttails into his trousers. When he turned back to them, adjusting his trousers, Jessica asked, "Tell me, Mr. Frey, why do you call yourself *Executive Surveys?*"

"Oh, that? Well, I only talk to the top executives, not the secretaries." He smiled, and suddenly he didn't look at all alien to Anna, but rather like a bright young man trying to get ahead, who had a wife, two kids, and a house in Westchester. With the white shirt and the tie on, she couldn't even remember the pale hairy flesh and the washed-out undershirt underneath.

"Do you trail husbands?" Jessica asked, grinning.

"Everybody always asks that first," Frey said. "I wonder why."

"Well, do you?" Jessica insisted. "Do you trail men when their women want something on them?"

"Why don't you ask about tailing women so their men can get something on them?"

He put his jacket on, tucked the holster away carefully so that even to Anna's eye, knowing it was there, it was invisible. "Mae'll be along in a couple of minutes," he said.

She was. A fat blonde in a loose green coat came in, grunted at Frey, and asked if they were the girls Carol had called about. They nodded and stood up. "C'mon," she said.

"S'long, Mae," Frey called after them. "S'long, girls."

"You know what you can do, Bill," the blonde called back. She led them down the corridor to her door, opened it, and let them precede her. When she followed them inside, she left the door flung open behind her. The room was an old high-ceilinged office with a huge unshaded and uncurtained window that ran from floor to ceiling like a glass gash in the wall. Racks of colored dresses lined the gray room and gave the only brightness it had. Left of the window a shipping table, a desk with a telephone on the wall above it, and a sewing machine sat in a carefully shaped U, as if whoever sat at the desk in the center had fortified herself against attack from both sides. Except for a few cane-bottom chairs and a full-length mirror against the wall, the room was bare. Everything seemed dull, covered with a film of gray and mousy brown, as if the place had only been recently cleared of cobwebs that somehow had been rubbed into the walls for coloring.

Mae Rumage dropped her coat on a chair and Anna saw a mountainously fat woman in a tight black dress, obviously without underwear beneath. Embarrassed for her, Anna turned her eyes away. When she looked back, the older woman's bleached blonde head was tilted to one side, one of her eyes lost in the fat folds of her face, looking them over consideratively. For an instant Anna thought she might be winking. Then the woman said to Jessica, "What's your name?"

"I'm Mrs. Carruthers, and this . . . ."

". . . no, honey, your first name. We're friendly here."

"Jessica."

"And you?"

"Anna."

"Anna what?"

"Anna Townsend."

"You ain't no Missus." She said it as if she were certain, as if, unerringly, she knew that Anna was unmarried. She didn't even wait for Anna's corroborating nod. She simply knew.

"Okay," Mae said. "You can call me Mae. Anna, you stand over there. Jessica, you sit down here and I'll show you some of my pretties."

The dresses Mae had were lovely and she showed them to Jessica first, keeping up a running chatter with Anna while she did so. Jessica had warned Anna that they were to tell how poor they were because Mae always charged what the traffic would bear, and so, when Mae asked what they did, Anna told her they were poor social workers. No sooner were the words out of her mouth than Mae Rumage snapped her fat ringless fingers and said, "My God, I almost forgot. Glad you reminded me. You chickens will excuse me. I've got to make a call. I got to get my sister out of the bughouse. She was a little off her trolley, but they're letting her out tonight." Mae walked to the phone and then turned and called, "Say, one of you got some change?" Jessica gave her a dime, and for the first time Anna saw that it was a pay phone, looking incongruous on the wall.

When she had finished telephoning, Mae came to the racks where they were examining dresses, and said, "Well, chickens, do you like my dresses?"

"They're lovely," Jessica said.

"How about you?" Mae asked.

"Well, Mrs. Rumage. . . ."

"Call me Mae," she said, her voice commanding, not requesting. "What are you looking for?"

Anna told her about the red dress, trying to make it sound like a casual interest. She had seen a dress she wanted in a Fifty-seventh Street shop. When Mae asked where, Anna gave her the name of the place, saying that she hadn't bought the dress because it was too expensive. Jessica had suggested that perhaps Mae could get it wholesale for her, but Anna wasn't sure that she could.

"Of course I can get it," Mae said, looking insulted. "I've got special pull. I used to be a big-time model. I can get sample dresses from the best houses because they all know me." She patted her hair. "I can get any dress I want."

Anna gave her the rest of the details of the red dress, wondering all the while how such a mound of fat could ever have been a model. Yet, she did have a pleasant face, with good features under the fat, and perhaps her figure had once been good too. Her dark eyebrows and gray eyes were striking, almost hypnotic, and as Anna told her about the dress, she had the feeling that Mae sensed how important it really was to her, knew it in spite of the fact that Anna had spoken of it as matter-of-factly as possible, fighting the urgency she felt out of her voice.

When she was finished, Mae turned to Jessica. "You gonna try these on?"

Jessica nodded, still looking at the dresses she had picked from the racks.

"Well, go ahead then."

"Isn't there a dressing room?" Jessica asked.

"Do you see one?" Mae asked. "This is all there is." Majestically, she waved her arms around the room.

Jessica lifted her dress over her head, laid it carefully on a chair, and began to try on the dresses. Mae brought her others, recommending each in the most glowing terms, and, each time Jessica undressed, looked at her slim, high-breasted body with envious longing. Mae helped Jessica in and out of the dresses, touching her whenever she could. To Anna there was something sick and ugly about it, and the little remarks that accompanied the stroking. "You've got a lovely figure, chicken." "That's a good bustline, Jessica." "This one shows off your pretty hips." Jessica finally bought two dresses, a blue boucle and a bright plaid jersey, and looked lovely in both.

"And you?" Mae turned to her.

"I came for the red dress," Anna said. "I really can't afford any more."

"Don't you like my things?" Mae said, almost threateningly.

"Yes, I think they're lovely," Anna said, honestly, "but. . . ."

" . . . but me no buts." She drew two dresses from the racks and said, "Come on, try these. We'll find a couple just right for someone with your figure."

Reluctantly Anna took the two dresses from her hand, feeling that Mae wanted more to see her undressed than to have her buy the dresses. She took her jacket off, her blouse, and stepped out of her skirt, watching Mae's eyes as she stood there in half-slip and brassiere.

"You've got something there," Mae said admiringly, looking at her bust. "I used to look like that," she continued, as if waiting for someone to contradict her. Someone did.

"I'll bet you did, Mae, but that was sure a hell of a while ago."

Anna saw the detective, Frey, in the hallway, looking her up and down. "She's dead right though, sister. You sure got what it takes." In the air his hands made the rounded motions of breasts and hips, and Anna, suddenly aware, covered herself with a dress.

"On your way, Willie boy, before your eyes pop out of your face," Mae said. "G'wan now, save your buttons."

"If you ever change your mind about that drink," the detective invited Anna, "just let me know. Or you either," he turned gallantly to Jessica. He tipped his brown fedora, mock-bowed to Mae, and then they heard his heels clack down the corridor toward the elevator.

"Don't you think you ought to keep that door closed," Jessica said.

"Too stuffy in here. Ventilation's no good. Besides, nobody but Bill Frey and maybe that elevator boy passes."

"Is that all?" Anna said, trying for the right sarcastic tone, but Mae seemed to miss it.

Anna tried on one dress after another, feeling Mae's slithering hands helping her, holding her. She felt a sudden quaking terror, as if she was walking along a steep cliff in a heavy mist and couldn't see her way. She might walk off the edge and into the surf she was sure she heard surging against the rocks somewhere below, but she didn't know which way the lip of the precipice was and so she couldn't know how to turn. The hands always seemed to brush her naked skin, casually, helping her in and out of dresses, caressing her arm, her back, her shoulder, once just flicking the edge of her breast, almost probing into the recesses of her heart, so that it set the sound of surf going in her mind and in her flesh. Finally, almost without looking, and knowing that she couldn't afford it, Anna chose a green crepe with piqué collar and cuffs so that she could get it over with. Then she got back into her own suit.

After they had paid, Mae asked for a deposit on the red dress, but Anna had no money left. She knew she shouldn't have bought the green crepe; she hadn't wanted it, but because it seemed that Mae would never let her go and stop touching her until she bought something, she had taken it. Anna promised to mail her a check that

evening and they left with the smell of Mae's ginny breath hanging
in the corridor, and the sound of her "Goodbye dearies" following
them to the elevator.

In the street Jessica broke into burst of laughter. "Why . . .
why . . . you look like you've seen a ghost."

"I feel like it," Anna replied, trying to smile. Automatically, she
looked up at the darkened building, where only one window was
lighted. "Look!" she exclaimed, pointing to the lighted window of
Mae Rumage's shop where big letters that ran horizontally across
the middle of the window spelled out *DRESSES*, and smaller letters
in the lower corner said *Rooms.* As they were watching, the window
went dark.

"I wonder what that means," Jessica said. And, after a minute,
"It was weird, Anna, wasn't it?"

"That's the understatement of the year."

"Did you see the way that detective leered at us. I thought he'd
start drooling any minute," Jessica said, lapsing into helpless
laughter.

"You expect that from him, but her." Anna shook inside as the
prickling of her scalp and skin and the sound of the surf in her head
ran through her. "How she touched me!"

"Me too. I thought she was enjoying it a little more than the line
of duty called for," Jessica said soberly. "You think she's. . . ."

". . . I don't know what she is," Anna said, uneasy about being
asked to label Mae Rumage. "But whatever she is, I don't like it.
She frightens me."

"What's there to be afraid of because a fat old ex-model gives you
a couple of pats? You get worse any morning in the subway rush."

"This is different, Jessie. This woman's—I don't know how to
say it without sounding ridiculous, or hysterical—but she's evil."

"Whoa! Anna! That's pretty strong."

Anna didn't answer. The woman had some strange power,
something she couldn't explain. The oddly clear gray eyes under the
absurd black eyebrows, so unlikely in the fat, pleasant-looking face;
those eyes and the power that leaped from the sloppy fat body made
her take that green crepe, although she didn't need it and couldn't
possibly afford it. Yet she had bought it. Why?

At the corner they waited for the light to change and when they started across the street, Mae's voice came suddenly from behind them. "Watch out for the cars, dearies. Don't get run over." They turned and saw her coming down the street, surprisingly light and swift. She waved and said, "And tell all the other girls about my beautiful dresses. Don't forget."

Together, like a small chorus, Anna and Jessica said in unison, "We won't," and then Mae had turned the other corner and disappeared into a doorway.

At her apartment, Anna was too unnerved to prepare or eat dinner. Something was racing inside her like a car with its brakes on. Instead of eating, she poured herself a whisky to quiet her nerves and sat down in the living room to figure it out. Between sips of whisky she told herself that she was acting like a child, giving in to a whim about a dress and frightened of a harmless fat old lady. Let's break this down, and analyze this, she told herself. What's bothering me anyway? I don't really need that red dress any more than I needed the green crepe. What's more, I can't afford either of them. But I want it, the racing inside of her purred. But why? she asked herself, despairing of an answer. I want it and that's all, the racing said firmly, brooking neither question nor argument. Because she was unused to drinking, the whisky fogged her brain, and just before she fell into unquiet sleep, Anna wondered what was happening to her.

The next day Anna had the afternoon off, for she was on night duty on Friday, so she went shopping. She ransacked the small shops and the big department stores, but she couldn't find the red dress, and she hated herself while she searched. When she got back to her apartment, she was exhausted but she kept seeing the red dress flowing silkily against her body. When she awoke the next morning she felt as if she had not slept. She had had nightmares but what they were she couldn't recall, and she remembered she had forgotten to mail the deposit check to Mae Rumage. At lunch, Anna called and told Mae the check would be in the mail that afternoon.

"I'm sure glad you called, dearie, because I found that dress. Just like I said I would. I thought maybe you forgot."

"No, I didn't forget," Anna said, trying to be casual but hearing her own eagerness. "When can you have it for me?"

"If I get that check tomorrow, I'll have it in a day or two."

"Are you sure?"

"Soon as I get it, I'll call you. But first you mail that check," Mae said, businesslike.

Although she mailed the check that evening, it wasn't until Friday that Mae called. It was late in the afternoon, almost four, when the switchboard operator called Anna to say a Mrs. Rumage was on the phone. "Hello, Anna?" Mae's voice was metallic and distant.

"Mae? This is Anna. Have you got the dress?"

"Sure. I got your size too, so we won't need to alter it. You bring fifty bucks and it's all yours."

"But I sent you a check for twenty-five."

"The dress is seventy-five, and that's a good price. If you want it, come right away."

"I can't. I work late tonight, until eight."

"Bring cash."

"Where'll I get cash now? The banks are closed. Can't you take my check?"

"Cash, or no dress."

"Where will I get it?" Anna wailed, hating herself for not saying never mind the dress, and for the subterranean cry in her voice.

"Borrow it. Ask the girls. You want the dress, get the cash."

"All right, Mae," Anna said wearily, "I'll be there."

It took her until the time she left to get the fifty dollars. Anna was embarrassed, but she borrowed from the switchboard operator, from another of the social workers, from one of the residents she knew well and from an interne she didn't know at all, and even from Fannie, the washwoman.

When she finally got up to Mae's, it was very dark. Mae's window was lit, illuminating sharply the words *DRESSES* and *Rooms,* so that they seemed to have been carved into the light. The elevators were not running and Anna had to walk up the five flights, holding herself from rushing, because even if she couldn't wait for the red dress, something inside her knew that she must not let herself be carried away. She passed William Frey's *Executive Surveys* and smiled when she saw the light dim from the second room, with the bed and the liquor buffet. He didn't believe in working late he had told her, nine to five for him.

Mae's door was open and when Anna walked in there was only a little dark-haired woman sitting at the shipping table, carefully wrapping dresses. "Hello," Anna said, "is Mae in?" The woman did not look up. Her face was blank, the black eyes remote and expressionless, the mouth an unsmiling line. She said nothing, but she went on wrapping. Schiz, if I ever saw one, Anna thought, picturing the ones she had known. She remembered Mae's phone call the day she and Jessica had been there. This must be her sister, the one she was getting out of the "bughouse," Anna speculated. The woman didn't look like she should have been let out. She went on packing. She picked up a dress, folded it neatly into a cardboard box she took from the floor next to her, closed the box, and tied it with cord. As she finished tying each box, she snapped the cord between her fingers, her knuckles going white with the effort, but separating the cord from the spool before she dropped the finished box into a pile on her other side. Everything was in its place: a pile of dresses on the table, a pile of boxes on the floor, a roll of cord next to the dresses, all in easy reach. Watching made Anna nervous and she took out a pack of cigarettes and offered one, but the woman did not even acknowledge the existence of her outstretched hand.

"Well, if it isn't Anna." The booming voice behind her was close and Anna dropped the cigarette she had begun to light. It was Mae. "I didn't think you'd get here." Abruptly, as Anna was bending to pick up the cigarette, and almost leaping from place to place, Mae began to show her dresses, one after the other, style after style, color after color: blues and greens and yellows and reds, seeming to bring the clothes not only from the racks, but from the floors and walls and ceiling, and even out of her own big flabby body. Mae's black brows were unruffled but her gray eyes were shining with excitement and there was a film of sweat beaded on her upper lip as she displayed dress after dress. "The finest gowns in town. From the best places. You can see the labels." But Anna didn't see a single label. Every dress was placed against Mae's huge body so that each seemed slender against the gross black-dressed bulk behind. Each dress was the most beautiful, the one for her, Mae assured Anna, just what she needed to show off her best features. And with each Mae asked in an urgent, sensuous voice, "Aren't they beautiful? Have you ever seen such pretties? They're so lovely, my gowns, the loveliest," commanding appreciation, demanding response.

"Stop. Please stop," Anna cried, surprised at the loudness and intensity of her voice in the quiet room. "Don't show me any others. Please. I can't afford another dress. I can't afford any dress. I only want the red one and that's all."

There was a moment of silence and Mae said threateningly, "Don't you like my things?"

"Of course I do, but I can't possibly afford them."

Mae looked at her as if stunned, and then, curiously reasonable, said, "You don't have a chance to wear many clothes in your job, do you? What did you say you do?" Anna told her about social work. Mae kept plying her with questions, some she had asked before, some she kept repeating two or three times, sometimes at intervals, other times in succession. Where do you work? What do you do? Do you like to go out? Do you go many places? Where? Do you like pretty clothes? Do you have a nice apartment? Anna listened to herself giving Mae answers, picturing herself as a deprived unhappy girl who wanted another life, a life filled with going out and fashionable apartments and a red dress, and all the while she heard these answers, as if another distant, yet intimate, part of her spoke for all of her, Anna wanted to cry out, "I'm not like that at all. That's not what I want. I've got a good and full life." But somewhere the cry was stifled inside her. Mae stood there listening, nodding her head understandingly, but Anna saw the calm gray eyes measuring her, estimating her.

When Mae spoke, her voice was like oil on waves, soothing and deceptively calm. "I like you," she said, her eyes widening until the pupils looked large and blacker. "Maybe I'll give you some of my dirtied and mussed-up dresses for free."

"No. You mustn't do that," Anna said, feeling like a fool and a liar for having painted a picture of herself and her life that was so untrue. It was as if there were things she was feeling for and did not grasp, as if she was stumbling forward for solid ground that she would never again walk on, and she felt she was falling into the bizarre depths of those gray eyes and widening dark pupils, depths in herself from which she could never return.

"Now don't you worry, dearie. I like you and when I like someone, I like them. You want pretty things, don't you?" Mae asked for the fifth or sixth time, and, not waiting Anna's answer, plunged ahead. "Look, I tell you what. I've got a friend who has lots of nice clothes and wants to give them to someone nice . . . like you."

"How about my red dress?" Anna asked.

"Oh that," Mae said, casually turning to her desk. "I didn't expect you with the money. That rich friend of mine came up this afternoon and she liked it so much, I sold it to her."

"You sold it!" Anna gasped, her breath hard and panting.

"Don't worry, chicken. My friend'll give it back to you for nothing. Save you fifty bucks. She never wears a dress more than once or twice anyway. She'll give you the red dress and lots of other pretty things. She'll like you."

"You sold it," Anna repeated. "You sold *my* red dress."

"Now here, I'll write you a note and you can run right over and get it tonight. My friend won't mind. She lives down at the Hotel Germania. It's only a few blocks away. Her name's Mrs. Burtis." She sat down at the desk and began to write. She looked up at her sister for a moment and asked, "Say, Lydia, what's Mrs. Burtis's room number? And her first name?" Lydia didn't answer but went on with the automatic movements of packing dresses. She seemed not to have heard. Mae twisted her head to look at Anna. "Doesn't know a damn thing. She might as well be dead." Then she turned back and began to write again.

Lydia, Anna thought, what a beautiful name. A name to wear with that red dress. Lydia.

Mae got up and handed her a note on her business stationery, neat gray bond paper, the left side embossed with MAE RUMAGE'S EXCLUSIVE CREATIONS, the right side with a neat column of four words: *Dresses, Coats, Suits, Gowns.* On the paper Mae had written in a big green ink scrawl: "Give the things to this nice girl." Mae was still talking but Anna could hear her only as if her voice was coming through cotton stuffed in her ears, or over the telephone on a very long distance call where the voice grows softly blurred and the words indistinct. She was saying: "You walk down to the Germania and the doorman in front of the hotel will be there. Ask him for Mrs. Burtis. He'll say he doesn't remember her, that there are a lot of Mrs. Burtises, and you'll answer that there's only one Mrs. Burtis. Then he'll give you her room number. I forget the number but it's on the ninth floor."

While Mae went on talking, Anna stared at the note. Why this sounds like a password, she thought. And this Mrs. Burtis thing, with the doorman, and my red dress, and the free clothing, and the ninth floor, and my red dress . . . why, it's all insane. Abruptly, she cut short Mae's flow of talk. "No. I couldn't go to anyone's apartment for clothes."

Mae stopped and stared for a moment, and then, in a sudden springing movement, she tore the green inked note from Anna's hand. Mae almost ran to the far side of the room and when she turned, her face twisted and her body shaking as if with sobs, she shouted, "You don't have to! You don't have to!" In slow, deliberate movements, almost like her sister's, she tore the note and let the shreds float to the floor in front of her, a little white puddle. They stood there for minutes, silent, facing each other across the room, the only sounds coming from the rustling movements of Lydia's packing. And then came the snapping of the cord as Lydia broke it between her fingers, and the sound of it was an outcry in Anna's heart.

When next she remembered, Anna was at the opposite end of the hall, past the elevator, facing a glazed door that read *Equity Company*. She turned back to the elevator and rang the buzzer furiously, again and again. It wasn't until she heard noises from Frey's office and from Mae's that she remembered the elevators were not running. She walked down the stairs, barely keeping from flinging herself down headlong. In the darkened streets she wandered, unable to tell which direction she was moving in, walking until her aching mind and her aching feet reminded her that it was time to go home. A policeman was standing at the corner and Anna went up to him. "Which way is east?" she asked. "I want to take a bus crosstown to the East Side."

The policeman looked at her and pointed a gray-gloved hand. "That way. There's a bus stop right here, but go up to the next one." He smiled and went on kindly. "Funny things happen in this neighborhood sometimes and it won't do for a young girl like you to wait in the dark. You'll be better off walking the few blocks and waiting in the light."

Anna thanked him and walked blindly off in the direction he had pointed when she saw she was on the same street Mae's building was on. She passed it, frightened by its face, thin and long, crowded between buildings, its sides pressed together as if in a vice. When she looked up she saw Mae's light on and the letters *DRESSES* and *Rooms,* only this time, without a moment's reflection, she knew what they meant. She remembered that she had left the deposit on the red dress with Mae and was about to cross the street when she saw the dark brows and gray eyes, the shreds of paper floating to the floor and the beauty of the red dress, and she heard the strange loveliness of the name Lydia. In the distance ahead of her, squatting on the ground in a patch of light from the street overhead, she could see a bus sign, looking like an outlandish marker, a black and white arrow stuck in the concrete, and she made herself walk toward it, thinking all the time of the dress, the dress. And then, suddenly and impulsively, she was walking back down the street toward Mae's, and as she saw the face of the building staring down at her, rigid and disapproving, she knew she had returned for the red dress.

The Animal Trainer

There was always the tense moment of self-consciousness when he entered a class for the first time, and Cohen was aware of it again, the silence sudden, the conversation suspended in mid-sentence.

He walked from the door to the desk, put his briefcase down, and wrote on the blackboard in a big legible scrawl: English Composition IX, MWF, Room 713, Mr. Douglas Cohen. When he turned to look at the class, the faces were blurred and indistinct, but he knew that he would soon be able to pick out individual features, and in a few weeks he would be able to connect faces to names. Cohen tried to spend the first lesson the same way each time: read the names from the class cards, ask for corrections of his pronunciation of them, and then, after assigning the short story text and the first half-dozen themes, he tried to explain the purpose of the course. It was a course in how to read and write more intelligently, and, he added wryly, because it always brought forth an uncomfortable titter, through those things to learn, perhaps, how to behave more intelligently.

The first assignment was an autobiography, a good choice Cohen had found, because it helped him to get to know them, and at the same time it made them write from their own experience, and, he hoped, got them better acquainted with themselves.

Cohen read the names slowly, taking care with the pronunciation, and the replies were soft, and, as usual, reluctant, almost as if they hesitated about identifying themselves. The last two cards had strange names, and Cohen read them even more slowly.

"Von Harnisch, Wolfgang."

"Yah, Herr Doktor."

For a moment, Cohen thought it was an attempt at a joke, a freshman playing the clown, but when he followed the voice to the man, sitting tall and erect in the very last row, older and more ravaged than a joking freshman could possibly be, Cohen knew it was not a joke.

"I'm not a doctor . . . yet," Cohen smiled, and the class shuffled uncomfortably, not knowing whether to laugh or look serious. "So just say 'Here.' " Van Harnisch nodded, his head bowing stiffly from the neck as if struck from behind at the collarbone.

The last card read, "Zilanko, Yakov," and the name belonged to a dark-eyed, pale boy who sat quietly near a window in the front row, almost without breathing, and whose "Here" was so feathery soft that Cohen almost missed it.

When he dismissed the class, the students rose, suddenly at ease and graceful, and Cohen watched them file out in twos and threes while he took his cigarettes out. "Mr. Cohen?" He turned and saw Von Harnisch moving down the aisle toward him, dragging crippled legs on the floor, the tall, spare body jack-knifed over two rubber-tipped yellow canes. Cohen felt the pity sting his eyeballs, and he remembered his own terrifying fear of being crippled in the war. For a moment he felt as if he himself was hunched over the canes, feeling the strain in his shoulders and the dragging of his legs; then the match he had lit singed the hair of his fingers and brought him to lighting his cigarette and quickly blowing the match out. When he looked up, he hoped he had pushed the pity and the fear from his face.

"Yes, Mr. Harnisch?" he said.

" —Von Harnisch," the voice corrected gently, the eyes remote and dark, the lips full and curved in what might have been, but for the twisted corners of the mouth, a smile.

"Well, what is it?" Cohen asked, feeling irritation inside him mix with and take the place of his fear.

"I am not native born here, and I do not speak English good." He stopped as if he had to reconstruct from the German in his head first. "You think I am successful?"

"Sure, why not?"

"I will maybe need your help." The lips smiled, but the eyes were distant, almost unseeing, and Cohen wondered what the boy was trying to say.

"Of course," Cohen said, making his voice hearty. "That's my job. It's too bad we don't have foreigners' language classes here, but I'll do what I can to help."

"Good," Von Harnisch said, with the little stiff-necked bow. "*They* said there was maybe trouble."

"Trouble?" Cohen asked. "What kind of trouble?"

Von Harnisch's eyes looked away from him to his cigarette, his shoes, and then finally to the rubber tips of his own canes. "Because I am . . . was . . . a German soldier," he said, fumbling for the right tense, his eyes suddenly meeting Cohen's, his face stiffening, his body almost snapped erect.

A Nazi, Cohen thought. A Nazi soldier. He fought down the leaping pity and terror inside him. Probably wounded in the legs or spine. Shrapnel. Again he could almost feel himself on the canes, crippled, and then clearly he thought, "Serves the bastard right." He felt his hands shaking and dropped his cigarette. "*They* told you?" he said aloud.

Von Harnisch's eyes wandered, then dropped, and he repeated as if by rote, "*They* told me," but his hands fluttered helplessly toward the empty chairs in the classroom. Then he leaned heavily on the canes and began to pull himself toward the door.

"What else did *they* tell you?" Cohen made himself ask, not wanting to ask or know, his eyes seeing only the hunched shoulders and the long thin legs that buckled under the torso. It was here, again, in his own country, in his own classroom.

Von Harnisch was framed in the doorway when he turned, his fists bulking white-knuckled around the canes. "They said *you* are a Jew," and Cohen could almost feel the change of emphasis in the pronouns like a blow. Then he was gone, the sound of his dragging feet sibilant and threatening in the corridor. At his own feet his cigarette still glowed. Cohen picked it up, put it in his mouth, the dustiness of the floor dry on his lips.

"Even here," he thought again, "as if there are Furies following me from another life." Against his will, fighting back the sight and sound recalled, he remembered Dachau and Buchenwald, and the vivisection room—"for medical experiments," the Germans had said quite calmly—with its hooks in the ceiling for bodies to be hung from. He had picked up a worn mallet there, hefted it in his hand aimlessly, the wood smooth against his palm, until he noticed the flat head stained with brown dried blood. Then his fingers, with a mind of their own, had gone limp and let the mallet fall to the concrete floor.

He didn't often think of it anymore. Sometimes, when he did remember, his memory blurred the outlines so that it seemed like a book he had read, or a nightmare from his childhood, filled with the horror of the slaughterhouse scenes of *The Jungle* and the inscrutable injustice of *The Trial,* or like some of the newsreels he had seen after he had come home from Germany, grayed-out scenes that looked as if they had been sifted through ashes. "Human ashes," he thought, flicking the cigarette ash, "gone through a crematorium chimney."

Cohen picked up his briefcase, walked to the door and absently turned the lights out. In the hall, the dark-eyed boy was leaning against the wall, his eyes narrowed against the smoke that curled up about his face from the cigarette in the hands that moved restless and strange in front of him.

"They never forget, hah?" the boy said.

"*They?* Who?" Cohen asked, remembering the mallet and the smell, the murderous smell of incinerated flesh that still lingered in his head like an ache. As they walked toward the exit, Cohen tried to shake the smell out of his head by thinking about the boy's name, but he couldn't remember it.

"The Nazis," the boy said quietly. "The Germans."

"What do you know about that?" Cohen asked angrily as they came into the faded February sunshine.

They stood facing each other like contestants until the boy forced a laugh. "What do I know about it? Nothing. Nothing, I guess. Just what I read in the papers." The dark eyes darkened and the red mouth, almost fruit-stained looking, pursed. "Sorry I bothered you, Mr. Cohen," he said and walked away toward Bonner Hall, across the campus. Cohen watched him go with a vague feeling of regret, as if he had somehow misunderstood what the boy was trying to say. He tried to shake the feeling off. After all, what did that kid know about it anyway? Then he remembered the boy's name, Zilanko, Yakov. A foreign name. And there was the elusive trace of accent in the speech. Was the boy a refugee? No. That couldn't be. He couldn't possibly have learned English so well and so quickly.

At lunch, when he met John Summers, his best friend in the department, he told Summers about Von Harnisch and Zilanko.

"I'll take the pig-head off your hands, if you want me to," Summers offered, his thin, blue-eyed face detached and comfortable. "I've got a comp section that same hour."

Cohen considered it for a moment and then shook his head.

"You think you're going to reform a Nazi?" Summers smirked.

"No, it's not that."

"Then what is it? The best you can accomplish is to prove to him that you're a 'white Jew.' Big deal. That won't give him a twinge of remorse about the millions of Jews he and his buddies made into lampshades and burned for incense."

"And used for guinea-pigs," Cohen thought, still feeling the bloodied mallet in his hand, but he did not say the words. He sipped the bitter taste of the usual cafeteria coffee. He wanted to explain, but he didn't know how. The words he thought of were pompous or shopworn, and he didn't know how to make them say what he wanted to, so he let it go with, "Let me try for a while. If it doesn't work out, John, I'll transfer him to your class."

"Okay, Doug, but you're a sap for keeping him. He'll have some kind of respect for me because I'm a blue-eyed *goy*." He grinned at the unusual Yiddish word in his mouth. "And for me, he'll be just another Joe. But for you, he's going to be a Judas, or a crown of thorns." He looked up, his shrewd eyes narrowed. "Or is that what you want?"

For the first week, Von Harnisch was like all the other students, reserved and unprepared. The second week, when the class handed the autobiographies in, Cohen was impatient to read Von Harnisch's and, because of his impatience, kept the paper for last. He felt, somehow, that the autobiography would be the second skirmish with Von Harnisch in a battle already joined. But he knew that the battle he had joined was not only with the German; it was with himself. When he had come home from Germany, he had deliberately laid the problem aside. He was not a statesman, he told himself—he was a schoolteacher. But the problem would not stay put, any more than the Belsens and the Auschwitzes would remain quiet. The corpses cried out, and the mallet memory remained bludgeoned in his brain, and always he wondered what he would have done; kept quiet, gone about his business, and like the vast majority of them made believe there were no camps, no crematoria, no horror? Or would he have *resisted?* And how did one *resist?* Once, when they talked about it, Summers had said: "In any critical time, most people shut their doors and wait until the crisis is over." With tyranny and liberation alike.

Two or three papers before Von Harnisch's, Cohen came on Zilanko's paper, entitled "Zilanko's Journey."

It was written in restrained sentences, simple and compound, rarely complex, and in good idiomatic English. Zilanko had been born in Poland, in Lodz, in 1930. His father was a physician, his mother a concert pianist. Both of them had been educated in England and they had taught the boy English as a child, and continued to use it as the second language in the house after Polish. Zilanko was an only child, lonely because his parents were busy and had to leave him much of the time with Magda, the servant girl. Zilanko wrote how he had tried for their attention one day when he stole six zlotys from his mother's purse and treated all the kids in his gang to candy and a droshky ride around the town. But the principal of the school had seen him and reported the incident to his mother, and Zilanko had gotten the kind of attention he didn't want.

Cohen laughed out loud at the story, picturing the small, dark-eyed boy directing the droshky driver through the main streets of Lodz, where the principal had spotted them. It seemed like another world, a world of innocence and beauty long since gone. And soon the other world arrived, the world of September, 1939, when the

Nazis invaded and his father had been called up. Dr. Zilanko had sent the boy and his mother into the country to stay with relatives. Six weeks later the doctor's regiment was wiped out by the panzers.

The boy and his mother had been taken into Germany when the roundup of Jews was begun, to East Prussia, to Bavaria, to the Ruhr, and finally to Buchenwald where Mrs. Zilanko, weak and sickly, had been cremated. In 1945, Zilanko was liberated by the Americans—why the Nazis hadn't cremated him he wasn't sure, but he suspected it was because he could still work. Then his father's only brother, in America, had found him through the Joint Distribution Committee and brought him to the United States. Zilanko himself wanted to go to Israel, but his Uncle Max prevailed on him to remain until he finished work at the university and became a doctor like his father.

When he put the paper down, the sheets going white and blank before his eyes, Cohen fumbled blindly for a cigarette. When he lit it, he didn't smell the comforting odor of tobacco. The gray burnt-flesh odor seemed to fill his head instead. And he had been short with the boy when Zilanko had tried to talk to him! The boy hadn't spoken to him since, except when called on in class, and then, reply-ing as briefly as possible, he had avoided Cohen's eyes. Cohen felt sick. He went to the cupboard for a drink, but the bourbon didn't wash the smell or the taste away.

And suddenly, as he picked up Von Harnisch's paper, the hatred was black and bilious in him, and his fingers trembled with the urge to tear the paper once across, and then again, and again, until the bits fluttered white to the floor. But instead he put it down on his desk and began to read.

It was briefer than the others and titled "The Life and Work of Wolfgang von Harnisch."

For a moment, thinking of the usual Germanic scholarship of the graduate schools, and their lives and works of, Cohen smiled. They were so thorough, so efficient, that even his American teachers had felt themselves distinguished when they were referred to in the foot-note of a German scholarly work.

Von Harnisch had been born in Hamburg in 1924, where his father, an experimental physicist, worked for one of the big industrial firms. In 1934, after his father joined the National Socialist Party, Wolfgang and his brother Hans had entered the Jugend. Theirs had been a pleasant childhood, with skiing trips to the Tyrol and Norway, and bicycle trips to Italy and through the Rhine Valley. After his brother was killed in 1942—Hans was in the Afrika Korps—Von Harnisch had volunteered first for the Luftwaffe, and then, changing his mind, had gone into the Elite Guards instead. When he left for the Russian front in 1943, his parents could not see him off because they were at Pœnemunde, where his father was working on experimental rockets.

Von Harnisch had fought on the Russian front until well into 1944, when, having been twice wounded and decorated, he was transferred to the Western front to, as he put it, fight the Americans. There he was wounded and decorated again. In 1946, his father had been brought to the United States to help the United States Navy to develop guided missiles, and the boy and his mother had gone along. In California, Von Harnisch had found work as an animal trainer, work he loved, but when his father had been sent East to work with one of the larger aircraft firms, Von Harnisch, at his parents' urging, had accompanied them and returned to the university.

Cohen put the paper down and went for another bourbon. The hatred inside him was knotted in his throat and chest so that his breathing came hard, and swallowing was painful. But what good is it? he almost cried out to the empty room as he paced up and down. Still, he knew that hatred was healthy and has an astringency and meaning of its own if well directed. And besides, was there any alternative to hatred?

It wasn't until the third week in March that Cohen was able to make appointments with Von Harnisch and Zilanko. Appointments were for fifteen-minute conferences in which Cohen went over the students' papers—more valuable by far, he had found, than all the red pencil marks about structure, diction, spelling and punctuation he made in the margins of their papers. He tried to see every student in his classes at least twice a term in conference and, if possible, three or four times. Von Harnisch came in first, his dragging feet sounding in the corridor outside of Cohen's office, announcing his presence beforehand, and giving Cohen time to compose his face and fight down the hatred he felt rising. He turned his chair to the window, lit a cigarette, and called, "Come in."

The door opened slowly and Von Harnisch stood uncertainly on the threshold. "Come in," Cohen made himself repeat. "Sit down." Von Harnisch moved to the chair next to the desk, placed his yellow canes together against Cohen's desk, and then folded himself into the chair. "Smoke?" Cohen offered, swiveling to face Von Harnisch, but the boy shook his head and spread his papers on the desk. Cohen went over them line by line, explaining errors, making corrections, and occasionally and reluctantly giving explanations in German when Von Harnisch didn't seem to understand. Von Harnisch was inattentive and several times Cohen, bent over the papers, was aware that the boy was looking out of the window over his shoulder. Finally, angry, Cohen said: "Look here, Harnisch, this is for you, not me. I know all this stuff. If you're not interested, we can both save ourselves this time and trouble."

Von Harnisch was brought up short for a moment, and then, slowly and very distinctly, he said, "I have not wanted to go to school. I like on the outside to be."

"Then why did you come to the university?"

Von Harnisch showed his contempt plainly. "What else I could do . . . with these," he pointed to his sprawled legs, " . . . dance?"

Cohen turned to look out the window, noticing the peculiar diamond whiteness of the March afternoon lightening the blueness of the spruces outside, hoping to give the boy time to recover himself. Recover himself? The laughter inside was shrill. Recover? No one could be recovered, and why of all people should he care about a Nazi's recovery? Could Zilanko recover his father, or his mother, gone up in smoke from a crematorium chimney, without the dignity of burial, the grace of restoration to earth? Could the boy recover the beauty and innocence of those stolen zlotys and that droshky ride? After the silence, Cohen turned back and asked if Von Harnisch could still train animals.

"You see ever how animals train?" Von Harnisch inquired.

Cohen shook his head.

Leaning on one cane with his left arm, Von Harnisch lurched to his feet, brandishing the second cane in his right hand. "You pick up two by four, go into cage, with only two by four. When lion jumps, or panther or leopard, you hit with two by four." He swung the yellow cane viciously, whoosh-whiiish, whiish-whoosh. "Best on nose. He jump again, you hit again, until he knocked down. Then you hit more so he know you are boss. After, he is good trained lion." Von Harnisch stopped, his eyes white and alive, and looked down at Cohen. "Outside people think animals trained with soft hand, but impossible. Must use two by four, or you dead and animal wild."

Von Harnisch bowed into the chair, as if he had completed a performance, and Cohen felt the surges of nausea and pity together. He remembered the mallet and the dried blood on it, and the picture of it seemed to swim between him and Von Harnisch, and change to a two by four, and then back again into a mallet. To keep the dizziness down, he asked, "If you did it before, why can't you do it again?"

"Before?" Von Harnisch rasped. "Before I have legs." He slapped his thigh with an open palm, making a loud flat sound. "I get these sticks like this," and, as Von Harnisch explained, Cohen realized for the first time that the German hadn't been wounded in the war. He used to feed snakes and take out their venom until one day he'd been bitten. He didn't remember when, but suddenly he was paralyzed from the neck down. They took him to a hospital and told him it was a snakebite, or maybe another animal's bite. They weren't sure which. He would never get out of bed again, they said, but Von Harnisch did not believe them.

He had begun to try moving immediately, starting with the right thumb, and after a year had accomplished what the doctors said was utterly impossible: he had moved his entire right arm. After that, with the doctors' help, he had recovered the use of the top half of his body in the second year, but the legs would not respond to treatment. The doctors said he would spend his life in a wheelchair—better than being in bed, they reassured him. But Von Harnisch would not accept that either. Ten and twelve hours a day he had practiced with the canes until he had passed out on the floor, but always the next day, he was up and trying the yellow canes once more. But, he explained, sweat drops standing out on his forehead as if he was reliving the whole thing as he told it, that was the best he'd been able to do.

"There've been no further improvements." He was convinced of the hopelessness of his being able to walk again, ever. He was tired of trying, too. "So," the German concluded, looking out at the blue spruces to avoid Cohen's eyes, "I come to the university. Here, maybe, I learn to make living—something when I am sitting, where I need no legs."

He had courage, Cohen was forced to admit, and he knew his pity and grudging admiration compromised his judgment. Still, what could such a man do? If he wanted to make a living he had to do something at a desk, anything that would require. . . . "Listen," he heard himself say, "whatever you do, you've got to know the language. Without English, you can do nothing."

Von Harnisch nodded, and Cohen suggested tutoring. The German said he would be able to pay, and Cohen promised to find someone to help him. Then Von Harnisch stood up, irresolutely put his hand out, and said, in German, "You are very good to me. Thanks." But there was a question in the statement, and Cohen felt it in the handshake too. It said, Why are you doing this for me? I am a German, a Nazi. You are a Jew. And worst of all, Cohen didn't know the answer.

When Zilanko knocked, Cohen was still staring out of the window at the spruces, wondering why he wanted to help Von Harnisch. Zilanko came in and sat down, putting his papers on the desk. When Cohen swiveled to face him, he noticed how the dark blue turtleneck sweater accented Zilanko's pallor and dark eyes. The boy always wore clothing that was a little out of date, too, a little strange and shabby—as if it had been rescued from trunks hidden away in old, musty attics.

"There isn't much to say to you, Mr. Zilanko." Cohen began. "Your work is good—surprisingly good for someone here so short a time."

"I spoke English in Poland, Mr. Cohen."

"That's right," Cohen said, "I remember now. Your mother

about six million of their leadership from Krupp down to the SS boys, we might really have defeated them."

"—and become just like them ourselves," Cohen said. "How do you judge? Who'd do the shooting? You? Me? Zilanko would, and he'd become a Von Harnisch, or worse. Besides, how would we have acted if we'd been Germans?"

"Or European Jews?" Summers said.

His own reply hadn't satisfied him, and Cohen felt the logic and horror of what Summers had said, but he didn't know what to make of it. Would he have hated Zilanko, or killed like Von Harnisch? Walking home after his last class, mulling it over in his mind, Cohen met with what was almost gratitude the gray sheet of rain that curtained the streets. The rain, the grayness, and the leafless trees black with wet matched his feelings better than the morning's sunshine had, and they made him more bitterly aware of Summers' comments.

At midterm, Von Harnisch was failing the course and Zilanko was getting an A minus. Zilanko's papers were impersonal and intelligent, and deliberately withdrawn. Von Harnisch's themes were intense and personal, and his English was abominable. He had no command of grammar, usage, or vocabulary, and since he had discovered that Cohen knew German, he had taken to writing in German what he couldn't express in English. In the class discussions, Von Harnisch's comments on the short stories were straightforward, frequently incorrect, and often so arrogantly asserted that they cut off all further comment by the class. Zilanko's remarks were hesitant, delivered tentatively, and were usually perceptive enough to open up discussion.

Although Cohen was several times forced to caution Von Harnisch about classroom etiquette, the German boy continued to interrupt others, to speak without waiting for acknowledgment, and to make hoarse asides during others' recitations, while the class sat back in astonished politeness and watched. The three-cornered tension was obvious to the class, and it waited with an almost sadistic delight for the discussions to flow. Cohen knew but could not control. The arguments usually began with his own "Don't you think?'' followed by Von Harnisch's "No, Mr. Cohen, it is''—the *is* always emphatic—and finally, cool but persistent, Zilanko's "Perhaps, but also. . . .''

No one of them seemed to convince the other, or, for that matter, the class either, but none ever abandoned a position in the face of the others, and the class looked on the contest like Romans watching gladiators performing in the Coliseum, their thumbs always down. Cohen knew he had lost control of his class for the first time in his teaching career, and he did not see how he could regain it and still maintain the democratic way in which he conducted his classes.

When he mentioned Von Harnisch's classroom behavior to Summers at a faculty meeting, Summers said, "If you're looking for a metamorphosis in that pig-headed Nazi by treating him with decency and consideration, Doug, you're a bigger jackass than I thought. He's gonna think you're afraid to shut him up, a yellow Yid, and what's more, the class'll agree with him. Neither he nor they will know you're presenting the . . .'' he laughed " . . . Christian ideal in action. They'll just imagine you're scared.''

It was only a week before the end of April that the class discussion was on Thomas Mann's "Mario and the Magician.'' The students had found the story very difficult to understand, and Cohen tried to clarify its meaning for them by explaining it as an allegory of the rise of Fascism, with Cipolla, the magician, mesmerizing his audience as dictators mesmerized the mass of the people. Carefully, Cohen showed how the whip and the drinking and the testy nationalism were all part of the picture. Almost as an afterthought, he pointed up the obvious irony of Mann's picture of it in Italy, since only a few years after the story was written, the same disease was to come to his own country, Germany, where its brutality and horror were to be carried far beyond anything accomplished in Italy.

Zilanko raised his hand to point out that the story showed further the degradation which Fascism inflicted on its devotees, making them, symbolically, stick out their tongues at others, cater to class prejudices, ignore scientific judgments, and fall into states of what Mann called "military somnambulism.''

Von Harnisch's roar came like the cry of anguish from a wounded animal, and he staggered to his feet, hunched over his canes, and bellowing, "It was not like that! It was . . . *wundershön* . . . beautiful . . . I do not listen more to this. . . ." He began to drag himself out of the row.

"Sit down!" Cohen's command was stentorian thunder in the class, and Von Harnisch stopped in his tracks. "Sit down!" Cohen repeated, and for a moment they stood staring at each other, tense and rigid, until slowly, slowly, Von Harnisch sank back into a chair.

"We've had enough of your arrogance," Cohen said, feeling the blood pounding in his trembling hands and shaking throat. "I've let you talk, interrupt others, and make a general damned fool of yourself, because we believe in giving even fools the privilege of shooting off their faces. But now, by God, you're going to listen, because we also believe that democracy imposes on its citizens the obligations of being informed. And you're going to be informed right here and now."

He paused, wet his lips, and swept the class with his eyes, noting Von Harnisch's stony expression and frightened, angry eyes, and Zilanko's shining face in almost the same glance. But he didn't care about either of them now. He felt a sudden freedom and power, a calm certainty. "Nazism was a cesspool," Cohen began, "an utter abomination." He told them about the Nazi horror, from Lidice to Rotterdam, from Warsaw to Dachau. He told them about the hostages, the wholesale slaughter, the slave labor, the assignment to brothels, the systematic starvations and "medical experiments," the gas chambers and crematoria, and the twenty million dead they were responsible for, not to mention the wounded, the maimed, and the havoc wrought all through Europe.

"They were wild animals," Cohen concluded, "and wild animals sometimes have to be beaten to train them. We beat them back to their lairs with their tails between their legs, but that doesn't mean that they're domesticated yet. And I don't dare use the word civilized. It takes a lot longer, it seems, to beat the jungle out of a man than out of an animal. And if we can ever beat it out of many men in a country, or a society, I don't know."

When he came in to lunch, Cohen found Summers waiting for

him with a big grin on his face, his blue eyes lit with sardonic laughter. "Well, Douglas, I hear you bombed Berlin today, with blockbusters."

"Maybe, but that only destroys houses. It doesn't replace them with new ones," Cohen said quietly. "Who told you, anyway?"

"Oh, things get around. In fact, it spread around the school like wildfire, and the kids will probably elect you the favorite professor of the freshman class."

"Shows how little they know."

"I wouldn't say that. They all think you're *dedicated*."

"Your word, John, or theirs?"

"Theirs. Honest injun. And there are half a dozen other faculty members who have Von Harnisch in their class who're going to vote you a bonus."

Dedicated, Cohen thought. To what? To anger, or hatred, or bombing the Wilhelmstrasse? But there was a point to it, he was forced to admit. He now had control of his class again, and perhaps some sort of control of Von Harnisch, too.

In early May, Cohen made an appointment for Von Harnisch's second conference. When the German came into the office, Cohen noted with a remote sadness that the boy looked older and more ravaged still. His sallow skin was waxen yellow, and the hollows were deep and dark under his eyes. He did not look up at Cohen as he slipped almost helplessly into the chair next to the desk and dropped his papers down before Cohen.

"Is something wrong, Harnisch?" Cohen asked. He had to tell the boy that unless he passed the final exam, he would fail the course, and he was finding it difficult to find the right words.

Von Harnisch nodded, his head limp and unstrung as a marionette's. His Adam's apple leaped faintly in his throat, and when he tried to speak, no words came out. Faintly, syllables began to come, then words and phrases, in a stream. He had really tried, he said. He had worked. He was failing all his courses and all because of the language. His father had even hired a private tutor for him, but he just couldn't learn English.

Cohen said, "Be patient. You don't learn a language overnight."

But Von Harnisch said there was no more time. If he couldn't learn the language, he might as well quit the university.

"What will you do?" Cohen asked, touched in spite of himself, and half wishing the German would quit so he himself would be relieved of the problem of grading him. "What will you do to make a living?" and, he wanted to add, to make a life?

Von Harnisch shrugged feebly. He didn't know what he would do, he said, or what he could do. He didn't care.

"It's not the end of the world if you fail," Cohen said. "You can take the course over, and the others too."

Von Harnisch stared and shook his head slowly to and fro, so finally, so worn out, that Cohen really believed that such an alternative was impossible for him.

"But look what you did after that snakebite," he said, astonished to find himself encouraging the boy, fighting to make him hold on. "Look at what patience and hard work did then."

The head shook again. "For that it is too late," Von Harnisch said in German. "I am too tired to struggle like that again."

Von Harnisch shook his head once more and wavered to his feet, leaning heavily on the yellow canes.

"You know," Cohen said, getting up with him, "everything depends on the final examination."

"Everything?" Cohen thought. Was it more than merely the course and the German's career at the university? Unexpectedly, it seemed like a reckoning: it was almost life itself. "Whoa," he said to himself, "you're overdramatizing. He'll come back even if he fails," but even while he thought it, he knew he did not believe Von Harnisch would come back.

As the German was about to go out, he turned and Cohen called to him, "If there's anything I can do—"

Von Harnisch smiled. It was the first time Cohen had seen him really smile, and for a moment the face flashed blooming and youthful in the doorway. Cohen could see him in his *wanderjahre* on the Rhine and in the Tyrol and in Norway. As if on the instant English were impossible for him, the German said, in his own language, "You are a man, a fair man, Mister Cohen." And then, with the ef-

fort stark and painful on his face, he said in English, "A . . .
fair . . . man."

During the last weeks of the term, Von Harnisch was subdued. He
said almost nothing in class, and when he was called on he spoke
with new tentativeness and mildness. It was obvious from his theme
papers that he was making a renewed effort. He wrote only in
English even when he came to the most difficult passages, but
Cohen knew his English was still far below passing. Zilanko's face
had darkened into quiet jubilation that showed in his unobtrusive
certitude in class, in a new warmth in his papers. Cohen avoided
prolonged talks with either of them, feeling only a quiet numbing
sense of futility and despair that the springtime yellowing of for-
sythia seemed to mock. He even avoided John Summers because he
didn't want to talk about whether or not he would have to pass Von
Harnisch.

The English composition classes all took their final exam in the
auditorium on the last day in May, and after seeing his class settled
and started, Summers walked over to where Cohen was proctoring
his class.

"Well, Doug," Summers said, "glad it's all over?"

Cohen nodded. "Damn glad."

"How's the pig-head making out?"

"He's still got an F average."

"You gonna fail him?"

"I don't know. Haven't made up my mind yet." He didn't tell
Summers about his last conference with Von Harnisch.

"Well, if he's doing F work, that makes it easy. What's there to
make up your mind about?"

"About what the F really means," Cohen said.

"You want it to mean something?" Summers asked, smiling.
"To him or to you?"

"Wouldn't you, John," Cohen said, "want it to mean something
to both of us. Seriously?"

Summers shrugged, saw an upraised arm, and walked down the
aisle to give a student another examination booklet.

Late that night, marking the papers, Cohen left Von Harnisch's
paper for last. Zilanko's blue book was an A, and Cohen gave him a

final grade of A. Then Cohen read Von Harnisch's blue book twice, slowly and deliberately. The examination was a failure. On re-reading it, Cohen discovered a little note on the very last page, a note he had missed in the first reading. It was not addressed to him, nor was it signed by Von Harnisch, although it was in the German's oddly formal handwriting. It read:

"What matter? I fail."

Cohen stared at the line until it expanded and contracted in his vision, appearing and disappearing like a mirage. Was it an appeal for pity? the desolate awareness of failure? the questioning of a whole world order? Cohen read it again and still again, but the meaning of the four words was sealed off from him. Finally, he put the examination booklet away without grading it and went to bed. He couldn't fall asleep. "What matter? I fail." The words kept flashing through his mind like a neon sign on a dark street, casting shadows of confusion in his mind and filming everything with red neon glow. Asleep, he dreamed of Zilanko holding a blood-stained mallet and of Von Harnisch in a droshky. When he awoke, he felt confused and almost sleep-drunk.

At breakfast, he read Von Harnisch's paper all the way through again, right to the little four-word note. Then, in red pencil, he marked a firm passing grade on it. He entered the passing final grade—just passing—in his roll book and then on the registrar's grade sheet. He put the grade sheet into an envelope, addressed it to the registrar, and, after he had shaved and dressed, walked through the sallow June sunshine to mail it. For a moment, the khaki color of the mailbox put him off, but then he smiled, dropped the envelope in, and clanged the lid shut. It was done, over with.

At commencement exercises, Cohen was putting his hood on and trying to adjust it properly when John Summers came up. "Hello, Doug," he said, setting the hood in place. "I hear you passed the Dutchman." Cohen put his mortarboard on and adjusted the tassel. "Did he pass the final?" Summers asked, stepping back to admire Cohen's handiwork with the tassel.

"Yes. . . . Well, no, not really," Cohen said.

"Then why'd you pass him?" John asked, the blue eyes appraising, but not surprised.

"If you don't know by now, John, I can't explain it to you."

"Well, try. Make believe I'm a freshman. I'll be patient. Is it because he's crippled?"

"Which crippling?" Cohen asked, almost of himself. And then, "That's part of it, I suppose, but not all of it. It's . . . it's . . ." but the words about Von Harnisch not being Germany, about individual and collective guilt, about the necessity for judging but not for punishing, and about a job sitting down, wouldn't come out. Nor could he explain that Von Harnisch still understood force at least, and could be taught, could grow. But Zilanko, his victim, no longer felt anything but hate, no longer believed in anything but the comradeship of hate and suffering.

Summers laughed at his struggle for words. "Forget it," he admonished. "I think I'm glad you passed him." He put his arm through Cohen's and together they walked across the campus toward the football field where summer graduation exercises were held. As they passed Bonner Hall, Cohen saw Zilanko leaning against one of the Doric columns, smoking, and for an instant their eyes met. Zilanko flicked his cigarette to the pavement, crushed it beneath his heel, and then, as Cohen waved to him, the boy turned his back and walked into the building.

"Well," Summers said, "I guess he told you, huh?"

Cohen nodded sadly. He didn't blame the boy. He could understand Zilanko's hatred. But hatred was not enough, nor ever would be.

"Come on," Summers said, tugging at his robe, "let's go graduate another batch."

"Sure," Cohen said, "might just as well," and together they walked toward the football field.

The Pearl Fishers

David saw old man Vecchione for the first time in the front garden of the house, bent over turned-up clumps of webbed earth, and he did not look up when David, going to Hebrew school, passed. They had just moved into the old, two-family house and David liked the bigness and the way the house sat by itself, away from the others, with the gardens in front and back, and the spreading magnolia tree that had not yet blossomed. His father had not liked the move, although it was only a block and a half from their old apartment house, and said so to his mother. "Why must we move into *their* house, Leah? We cannot move among our own?"

"But Jakob," his mother had said patiently, the words in her voice worn smooth as white stones, "it is a good place and they are good people. There is light and sun all day and plenty of room for the boy to play."

"Play! Agh!" his father grated. "He is a boy old enough to be studying Talmud. He is too old to play like a child."

But they moved anyway and his father already liked the new house, even if the Vecchiones did live downstairs and were the landlords, because he had a room where he could keep all his books, and where he could sit by himself, or with his friends, and study. David too had a room where he could draw and read and do homework, a big room at the back of the house, far from his mother's and father's room, so he could get up early and make noise if he liked and sit and look out of the big double windows. And looking out was the best of all in the new house, for beneath the windows was a hoed field that his mother told him was Mr. Vecchione's garden. Beyond it was a long narrow strip of hard ground, beaten down by many feet, and outlined with a thin ribbon of wooden planks. There the old Italian men played a strange game with little black balls, rolling them from one end of the field to the other, running after them, and sometimes yelling and raising their hands in question or in triumph, their fingers all together, and their hands in the distance flitting like brown sparrows. After the games they sat around a wooden table just outside the borderline of planks, shaded by four twisted peaches trees and a faded orange umbrella that rose out of the table like a mushroom, drinking wine and talking, and sometimes watching others play the game.

On their first Sabbath in the Vecchione house, David came home and found his mother preparing the usual meal. The house had its special Friday night quiet, as if he would have to whisper to say anything. His mother moved silently about the dining room, setting the long, braided *chalah* on the round table, the log-shaped *kugel*, its odor of baked noodles and white raisins filling his head and making his mouth water; the gefilte fish, white and snowball-shaped, lay in a deep dish, and all of it shone on the icy-white tablecloth that was starched stiff beneath. His mother set the three-pronged silver candelabra in the center of the table, sparkling in the last light of the spring sunset, and put the white linen napkin on her head as she intoned the prayer of blessing the candles, moving her long brown hands over them in small circles that set the flames to shivering and set something shivering inside of him too. Something good, as if the house was filled with a white light that came from the fish and the tablecloth and the bright silver of the candelabra and its three flames, and David felt a lingering peace inside.

And the white quiet remained with him until his father, hungry and irritable from having waited so long for the evening prayer at the synagogue, came in. When they were gathered around the table and about to begin the Sabbath meal, they sang the ritual "Shalom Aleichem," the song he had always loved but that now seemed part of the whiteness and silence in him turned to melody that rose up pure and strong in him and floated out soprano over the food and candles.

> *Shalom aleichem, malache hashores, malache el yon.* . . .
> Peace be unto you, you ministering angels,
> Messengers of the Most High . . .
> May your coming be in peace . . .
> Bless me with peace. . . .

Not until he had finished the third stanza did David realize that his father and mother had stopped singing, and when he opened his eyes, they were exchanging looks and staring at him.

"Your voice," his mother said, softly and surprised, "why—it's beautiful."

"He sings like—," his father hesitated, groping for words, "—like a cantor." His father looked pleased and puzzled, as if suddenly he had found something precious in the street, where he had never expected to find it, and didn't know why he had been chosen to find it.

They stood there looking at him until David felt his cheeks grow hot and looked down at the shimmering table.

"Never have I heard you sing like that, David," his mother said, reaching toward him with a caress that smoothed his hair and straightened his skullcap at the same time. "You must sing some more for us."

"He must sing in the synagogue, Leah," his father said, "with the choir, on the altar. One day—who knows?—he will maybe be a cantor. Tomorrow I will speak to the cantor." His father smiled at him. "You would like to study with Chazan Barrt?'

David knew his father wanted him to say yes, but he couldn't. Nor would he say no. He looked down at the tablecloth again, anxious because it was the same voice he had always sung with, only he had not sung much before his parents. His father came around the table and put his hands on his shoulders so that David could feel his own blood beating against his father's palms. "You will sing like an angel, the 'Kiddush,' 'Neilah,' 'Kol Nidre,' like Yossele Rosenblatt." His fingers tightened. "My son, David." His father sounded proud of him, as he almost never did, and David was happy. But when they sang the last stanza together,

> May your departure be in peace, you messengers of peace,
> Messengers of the Most High, the supreme King of Kings,
> Holy and blessed is He.

the white quiet inside him had gone.

After supper David went out into the back yard and looked at the moon, white and quiet on old man Vecchione's field, but the feeling did not come back, and he felt only the pinch of the pickets of the fence as he leaned his arms between them.

The voice behind him was strange and hoarse, but it did not startle him when he heard it. Even without turning, he knew it was old man Vecchione.

". . . that was you, upastairs, singing?" the old man asked. David nodded.

" . . . you sing vera fine. You study musica?"

David turned and was surprised to find the old man's face; the quiet gray-blue eyes like marbles in the wrinkled sand of the face, on a level with his own because the old man was bent over like a jackknife with the blade left half-open. That was the way he stood and walked. "No," David said, "I do not study music."

"You like?" he asked, the full chapped lips suddenly smiling, and David knew he meant the music, not the study.

"I like," David said, smiling back.

"Come," the old man motioned for him to follow, and then, abruptly, he turned and said, "Whatsa you name?"

"David."

"My name is Vincente Vecchione, but everyone callsa me Pop. You calla me Pop. O.K.?"

"O.K.," David laughed, " . . . Pop."

Pop led him through the back entrance of the house into the cellar. There, under a dim, green-shaded yellow bulb that hung over a table, four men were playing cards. "Those my sons: Joseph, he'sa the oldest, and then Vito and Carmine. The other, he—how you say it?—stay with us. Rent a room upstairs. His name John Strigari." He called to the men in his rasping voice, "Hey, boys, thisa here is new boy lives upstairs. David."

They waved and called hello, but did not look up from their game. David followed Pop past the staircase that led up to the Vecchiones' apartment on the first floor, and walked into a front room furnished like a parlor, with a rug and a couch and big victrola. The old man went to the victrola cabinet and opened it, almost patting the dark polished top into place. Painted on the open cover, David saw a black and white dog sitting next to a megaphone. "This machine could be you best frien," Pop said, talking almost to himself. "When you sad, it makes you music so the sad is easier, and you be happy by and by. When you tired, it make you rest. Is a ver good frien." He motioned. "Come ona here. I show how she works."

Carefully the old man explained and David watched how the victrola was to be wound with the metal arm that came out of its mahogany side, how new needles were to be taken out of a little metal pit and put in the head of the phonograph arm, how the old needles went into another little pit, and finally, how the shiny black record with the red label was set on the felt turntable and the arm and needle brought gently down on it. "Is Caruso," Pop said, putting the first record on. "A big record. The biggest. He's tenor. You listen, eh?"

David nodded and sat on the old couch. First there was only a little scraping sound, like a cat scratching the door at night, and then the music came, and a slow sad lonely crying voice, and David forgot the scratching and the dusty smell of the couch and the sounds of the card players in the next room. He even forgot about Pop, standing next to the victrola, his white head lifted from his doubled-up body as if it no longer belonged to it. And David felt as he sometimes did when he ran wildly down the streets into the wind, the air rushing against his face and into his lungs, until he felt he was flying. All he could hear was the rising and falling of the voice, its turning in and flowing out, loud, soft, in words he did not recognize, but speaking a language he knew without words, a speech that ran through him and lifted him like the wind.

When the music ended there was again the cat-scratching, then silence, and the old man, tears in his eyes, stood looking at him. "You like," he managed to say, without its being a question.

David nodded, not trusting his voice to speak for him, not wanting to break the other sounds with his voice, unwilling to come down
from the flying and the wind whirling. Never had he heard anything
like it. It was even better than the "Kol Nidre," or the "Umipenay
Chatoenu" in the synagogue.

"Some day, maybe, you sing like him?" Pop smiled.

David shook his head. No other voice could ever be like that.

"But you try?"

"I will try," David said, finding his voice in his throat new and
trembling. "What is the name of the music?"

"I don know how you call him in English," Pop said, running
earth-color hands through his snowy hair. "Hey, Carmine," he
called, "how you call tha music in English?"

"It's called the *Pearl Fishers* aria, Papa," a summery soft girl's
voice said.

"Oho, is Antoinette," Pop said, turning to the door. "Is my
daughter, the youngest, Toni."

In the doorway stood a tall young woman in a white dress, looking in the dimness like a fragment of the moon that had walked into
the cellar. David was surprised at the wild yellow of her hair and the
coal-glow eyes beneath. It wasn't until she came into the room and
took her father's arm, erect and lithe next to his gnarled body, that
David saw that she was only a girl, no more than fourteen or fifteen.
A light behind Pop Vecchione's face glowed when he looked at her,
proud and admiring, the way his mother sometimes looked at him,
and the old man's head seemed again to lift from his bent body.

"Toni, is the new boy from upastairs, David."

"Hello, David," Toni said.

"Hello, Toni," David answered, unable to look directly at her
moonlit beauty.

"Why you no sing for me and my Toni?" Pop requested.

"Don't be bashful," Toni coaxed in her summery voice, and
David knew he had to sing: it was as if he had swallowed a little piece
of her, her wild yellow hair and her quiet dark voice, that was a
song. Into his throat unbidden there came an old tune his mother
often sang, "The Three Sisters," and in Yiddish he sang:

> In England there is a town Leicester,
> In London is the same named square,
> And there we find three sisters,
> Of whose lives are none aware.
> The eldest she sells her bright flowers,
> The second sells laces for pelf,
> And late in the night we see coming,
> The youngest who sells only herself.

When he finished, Pop and Toni applauded together, and David could hear separately the thick calloused sounds of Pop's palms and the whisper of Toni's soft hands.

"What do the words mean, David?" Toni asked, her eyes dark-glistening and faraway.

"I don't know," David admitted. "It's just a song about three sisters in England. My mother always sings it."

"It sounds so sad."

"I guess it is. The music is sad, but I don't think the words are so sad," David said.

A sudden embarrassed silence settled over them, the only sounds the wax slap of cards on the table in the next room.

"Let's all go outside and look at Pop's tomato plants," Toni said quickly, extending her arm for him to take, and pulling her father along with her. "He's even prouder of them than of the victrola records."

Arm in arm, the three of them walked sidewise through the narrow doorway into the back room just as the Vecchione brothers and John Strigari were getting up from their card table.

"You through?" Toni asked.

"Your brothers weren't satisfied with the rent money your mother gets," John Strigari said—David noticed him for the first time, a short, slender man with hair so black it looked wet—"so your brothers decided to win some more playing cards."

"He'sa not so good witha cards, eh Vito?" Pop said. "Mebbe, Johnny, you betta stick by painting houses for living."

Outside, in the spring air that still had the chill of winter on it, they all walked to the picket fence that separated the back yard from the field beyond that was plowed with furrows of dark and light. Johnny Strigari lighted a crooked little black cigar. They stood silently for a few moments and then from behind came a new voice. "You keep you papa in the night cold and make bad his rheumatiz. You good sons and daughter."

They all turned together and David saw Mrs. Vecchione, short, almost square, but with the faded blond hair that must once have been wild and bright as Toni's, and with the same dark skin and eyes. Pop said something in swift Italian and they all laughed.

"You laugh," Mrs. Vecchione said, "but it'sa not funny."

"O.K., O.K. I go inside," Pop said. "But I like for you to know the upastairs boy, David."

"Hello," David said.

"You sing musica before?" Mama Vecchione asked.

"It'sa him all right. He sings like little Caruso," Pop said proudly.

"D—a—a—v—i—d!" His mother was calling and David realized how late it was. He let go of Toni's arm, called a quick good night to all of them, and bolted down the alley toward the front of the house.

In the morning David found Toni waiting for him next to the magnolia tree, which overnight had unfurled into a cloud of petals over the garden, and they walked together to school. Although she was almost two years older than he was, David was only a year behind her because he had skipped two grades, and they went to the same junior high school. That afternoon, when David came home from Hebrew school, Joe was in the back yard, leaning against the picket fence and watching the old men play the game with the black balls. "Hello," David said shyly, not sure that Pop Vecchione's tall, thin-faced son would remember him from the night before.

"Hi, David," Joe said, mussing his hair. "Where've you been all afternoon?"

"Hebrew school."

"Oh. I used to go to one of those when I was your age."

"Hebrew school?" David asked, surprised, trying to imagine Joe's dark Italian face in the synagogue.

"No," Joe laughed. "Catholic school, but we learned the same kind of things."

"Oh, but you didn't study Talmud and Gemara," David said, certain it was different.

"No," Joe laughed again. "What's it like in your school?"

David told him about the Hebrew school, about Rabbi Eisner and Rabbi Greenberg, and how he had been *bar mitzvah,* and how he was studying Gemara, and he would have told him more, but Toni arrived.

"I thought you were going to wait for me after school, David," Toni said.

"I didn't know you wanted me to," David said, remembering how he had hesitated and gone on alone because Toni was with some of the older boys and he was sure she didn't want to walk with him. "But I'll wait for you tomorrow," he offered eagerly, "—if you want me to."

"O.K., then, it's a date."

The three of them went into the cellar to the victrola room, and after Joe played the record twice, David sang with it the third time, singing only the melody of "Una furtiva lagrima," because he didn't know the words. Afterwards, Toni and Joe taught him to play an Italian game, *brisca,* and he won seventeen cents from Joe, but wouldn't take it, not even when Toni assured him that Joe was a schoolteacher and could afford it.

After that, David came to expect their walk to and from school under the arches of new spring-green trees, enjoying the way people turned to look at Toni and the way the other boys in his class teased about his "girl friend." As the silent spring days stole toward summer, David came to know the Vecchiones almost as well as his own family. Sometimes he almost wished he had been born into their family instead of his own, and when he did, he was ashamed and tried to be especially dutiful when his father asked him about Hebrew school, or when his mother wanted him to run an errand. With Mama Vecchione he always had fun. They sat together on the benches in the back yard and David helped her clean the snap beans and cut them, or peel and slice potatoes, or mix the dough for cakes, rubbing it the way his mother had taught him, while Mama Vecchione sang the old songs she remembered from Italy, songs that vaguely reminded him of the Yiddish ones his mother sang.

Sometimes he would sing her his mother's songs from the old country, because she would ask him to, and then ask her for the ones in Italian, the whirling dancing ones she told him were called tarantella, and the slow stately ones that were a little like the victrola records. She sang them all in a low breathy alto, like Toni's voice grown old, and he loved to listen. And always Mama Vecchione fed him, saying: "You gotta eat, David. You gonna be a big man." Although his father warned him about eating kosher food and often complained to his mother that he would become a *shagitz,* a *goi,* from being always with the Gentiles downstairs, David liked to eat with the Italian family. He did not tell his parents that he ate the thick, doughy, butter-colored macaroni and spicy red sauce, the crisp, beanlike chick-peas and salty anchovies, the earth-flavored lentils and bitter-crisp escarole, and the flat dry provolone. But he did not eat their meat, the unkosher ham and pork and bacon whose fat sweet smell made him sick.

In the dusky late afternoons Carmine and Vito played baseball with him after they came from work, and Joe sat in the back yard with him after school and read from books David had never heard of. But the stories and poems touched him, as the victrola music did, and he would lie on the wooden bench and listen to Joe's quiet voice read about other times and places. Sometimes, at night, they sat in the back yard, Vito with his concertina and Carmine with his guitar, and Mama Vecchione and he would sing, separately or together, in Italian or Yiddish or English, and Pop would clap his hands and stamp his feet, and Joe would drum with his fingers. Only Johnny Strigari, when he was there, was quiet, smoking his dark-smelling cigars. Toni would sing too, in her summery-soft voice, the lonely little Italian songs that hurt in his throat, and the others would grow quiet, their faces soft and open as they watched her. He knew they all loved her in a special way, perhaps because she was a girl, or because she was so beautiful, but in a way that made all their dark faces light when she sang and tossed her wild yellow hair. Once, Joe said that they loved her best because she was their hope; David asked him what that meant, but Joe only smiled and went back to reading him a poem. The way they looked at him when he sang was good too, and he knew they liked him, as he liked them, but with

Toni it was different, especially for Pop, who looked at her in a way he couldn't describe, except that he always seemed straighter when he did, and his old body seemed for a moment younger.

And it was with Pop he liked most to be. Sometimes, in the afternoons, David helped him in the garden, while the old man showed him corn and cabbages and his prize tomatoes. Or Pop took him to watch the old men playing the game with the black balls, called *bocci*, and even gave him a sip of the sour Chianti they drank. But with him David felt at home.

Other times he went to the Vecchione cellar by himself and played the old victrola and sang along with the melodies. Soon he knew the names on the records as well as the music: *La Traviata, La Forza del Destino, La Bohème, Il Trovatore;* but most of all he liked the *Pearl Fishers* aria, and he played the record over and over again until he knew it by heart.

One evening, when he had already eaten at the Vecchiones and could not get his mother's dinner down, his father looked first at him and then at his mother.

"He is eating unkosher food, Leah," his father said heavily.

David shook his head, not daring to speak, but he knew his father did not believe him. His mother, not speaking, took the plate from in front of him.

"Always he is down there with *them,* singing and making a fool of himself, just like *them.* He will grow up to be a taxi driver or a house painter."

David was surprised that his father knew Carmine was a taxi driver and Vito and Johnny Strigari were house painters. But why didn't he say that Joe was a teacher too?

"The boy is lonely and there are young people there. It is good. And he learns about the earth and planting from the old one," his mother said in his defense.

"And who will teach him Talmud there? And Jewishness?" his father asked, and no one answered. "They will teach him to sing their music, and for the holy songs his mouth will be unkosher and dumb."

David wanted to tell his father that he loved the cantillations, and the holy songs, that they were as sweet in his mouth and throat as the other music. But he was sure his father didn't care about that, as long as he could tell his friends that his son David sang with Cantor Barrt, and was even a soloist at weddings.

The week the magnolia tree's roof of white blossoms fell into the garden and petals skipped onto the pavements, David's father came home and said he was to study with Cantor Barrt. And so, in the afternoons, while the azaleas were red and then blew off in the spring winds and rains, David went to Cantor Barrt's house to practice. It was a green and white wooden house with a wide front porch where David waited until the cantor was ready and called him into the long, red-carpeted living room where he practiced scales and the cantorial melodies for the Sabbath and the High Holy Days, but most of all the songs that he hated, for the weddings: "I love you truly, truly dear . . . Because God made thee mine, I'll cherish thee . . . O promise me that some day you and I . . . When the dawn breaks in the sky, I love you. . . ." And Cantor Barrt accompanied him at the mahogany grand piano, correcting him, teaching him, but never quite talking *to* him, until David felt like a victrola the cantor had wound up and was listening to, his head tilted to one side, his gray hair showing beneath his black skullcap, his big curved nose quivering when he sang bass corrections to David's soprano mistakes.

When he finished, David raced home and into the Vecchione cellar to try to wipe away the memory of the wedding songs in listening to the victrola, or playing *brisca* with Toni, or Joe, or learning to play *bocci* with Pop and then help him with his tomato vines, tying them up on sticks. But it was like trying to drink the sour taste of Parmesan cheese out of his mouth with water, or even wine: he couldn't do it.

Often, when the spring was full outside, David lay awake in bed, tasting the sourness in his mouth and wishing he didn't have to go to Cantor Barrt's again. And one night when he could not sleep, he went and sat at the window. The moon was low and heavy and golden in the violet sky, and a pale gold mist was on the fields and the twisted flowering peach trees near the *bocci* alley. David opened the window quietly and leaned out, enjoying the soft wetness of the night air and the spring mist that had no chill. As he was looking up at the faraway specks of stars, he thought he heard rustling and a whisper light as the mist, and when he looked down, he was sure there were shadows in the stairwell that led to the cellar. For an instant, David thought there was a flash of yellow hair and he called "Toni?" in a soft, hoarse whisper, but there was no answer, and when he leaned farther out of the window, he could see no one in the stairwell.

In the morning, walking to school, David asked, "Was that you in the back yard last night?"

Toni turned to him, her face very straight, and then, in a minute, grinning and mussing his hair. "Now what would I be doing in the back yard last night?"

"I thought maybe you couldn't sleep, like me."

"I sleep fine," Toni said, "not like you. I don't have all your brains to keep me awake."

When the term was in its last week and Pop's tomatoes were red ripe on the vine, Toni was late one morning and they had to hurry. Halfway to school, her dark face went pale and loose and sick. Then, suddenly, she stopped and leaned over a garden hedge they were passing. David took her books and turned away as he heard her gasp. When she turned back from the hedge, her forehead glistened damp and her eyes were frightened. David wiped her forehead and her mouth gently and they stood together quietly, Toni, soft and still smelling of sleep, leaning heavily against him.

"You want me to go home with you?" David asked.

"I'll be all right in a minute," Toni managed in a hidden voice.

Walking home after school, Toni was quiet. David tried to tease and joke with her, as he usually did, but she didn't seem to hear him. After his singing lesson, he ran all the way home, but in the cellar Toni was in the victrola room with Johnny Strigari, her cheeks hot-looking and her yellow hair tangled. Even Johnny's wet-black hair was mussed, and when David ran in, he jumped up from the couch next to Toni and said, "Don't you ever knock before you come in?"

"What?" David asked, not understanding why Johnny seemed so angry.

"Nothing," Toni said. "Johnny's joking."

"Oh."

"It's having the afternoon off that makes him so funny," Toni said, smiling with a stiff mouth.

After a moment, David asked, "Are you O.K. now, Toni?"

Johnny wheeled, his usual little black cigar unlit in his mouth, a match flickering in his hand. "What?"

"Oh, it's nothing," Toni said. "Just the *scallopini* Mama made last night. I didn't feel so good this morning, so I threw it up going to school."

"No! God, no!" Johnny said. "Is that the first time?"

"No. That's what's funny," Toni said thoughtfully. "I've been feeling like that in the mornings now, every day, here." She placed her long tanned hand under her heart. "But it goes away after lunch."

"Holy Mother!" Johnny Strigari said. He threw his cigar on the floor and stamped on it with his feet, grinding the tobacco into the rug. "Holy Mother!"

The next morning while he was waiting for Toni to come out and walk to school, David saw Mama Vecchione coming out instead. Her face was stiff, as if she had just pressed it into shape with her hands before, and her eyes were swollen and red. "You no wait for my Antoinette," she said, not looking at him. "She no go to school today."

"Toni's sick?"

"Yes. She sick."

"Tell her I'll come see her after school," David said. "And I'll tell Miss Kendall she's sick and get her homework."

"You no see her. You no say nothing to teach'," Mama Vecchione said flatly. "She no go to school no more." Then the old woman turned, her eyes still faraway, and walked slowly back into the house.

David stood there, wanting to run after her and ask what was wrong. Was she angry with him? He had done nothing. At least he couldn't remember anything he had done. In school he couldn't sit still all day. He missed his recitation in Latin and got a zero for not paying attention in history, as well as a zero in algebra for not working two examples at the blackboard. That afternoon he couldn't concentrate on Cantor Barrt's teaching. When they rehearsed "O

Promise Me,'' he laughed out loud because again the cantor sang: "Those first sweet *w*iolets of early spring,'' and was so angry when David sang "*v*iolets'' that he hit David's knuckles with the baton he always kept on the piano. But the pain was less than what he had seen and felt in Mama Vecchione's face that morning. Toni was in trouble. Toni needed help. The Vecchiones were all in trouble and needed help. But what trouble he didn't know nor what he could do to help.

It was raining when he left the cantor's house and he walked slowly through the rain, letting it soak through his jacket and his hair and run down his face. The clouds were low over the housetops and it was almost dark when he slipped quietly into the Vecchione cellar. No one heard him. There, near the green-shaded yellow light, Pop and Joe were standing with their backs to him, and Carmine and Vito were holding Johnny Strigari facing them. Johnny's face was pale, his black hair plastered over his forehead, and one eye was closed and purplish. His thick lips were cut and his bared teeth bloodied.

"Why you do it?'' Pop was saying. "You live with us. We treat you like a son. Why? Why you had to do to us?''

"Aw, what's the use of talking, Pop,'' Carmine said. "Let Vito and me finish up what we started.''

"I no want you touch him,'' the old man said. "You unnerstand. I no want you put finger on Johnny. He gonna marry you sister.''

"You're crazy,'' Joe spoke for the first time. "He's no good. Send him away and we'll take Toni to a doctor.''

"He'sa no good. You right, Joe. But no take my Antoinette, my little girl, to doctor. He gonna marry—''

"That's what you think—'' Johnny began, but Vito hit him and Carmine held his arms.

The old man said something to Joe that David couldn't hear, and then to Vito and Carmine: "No hit him no more, I say.''

"But Pop,'' Joe protested. "Toni's a baby. She's not even fifteen yet. You can't make her marry. You'll ruin her life. She's too young.''

"Ina old country, is old enough to marry twelve year.''

"This isn't the old country,'' Joe insisted.

Johnny began to struggle, shouting, "I ain't gonna, you hear. I ain't. I ain't. She wanted to as much as I did. It's—"

The old man stepped up and slapped him, once, sharp across the mouth. "Shaddup. Shaddup. You hear. You no talk about my Toni. And no make so much noise. You gonna go upastairs now and tell Mama and Toni."

"Pop," Joe said, stepping between the old man and Johnny Strigari. "You just got to listen to me. You can't do this. Toni's your only daughter. You can't make her marry this . . . this. . . . She didn't know what she was doing," he broke off.

"No know?" The old man laughed, painful and rasping. "She not too young for—" he said something in Italian that David did not understand "—she not too young." There was a moment of quiet. "No more talk now. We go upastairs."

Between them Carmine and Vito forced Johnny up the stairs and Pop and Joe followed, Joe still talking, pleading, until their footsteps and voices faded into the apartment upstairs and David could not see or hear anything more. They had not even noticed him. For a long time David stood there in the puddle of rain that had dripped around his shoes from his wet clothing, trying to figure it out. Then he went out into the rain, around to the front of the house, and up to his own apartment. His mother was preparing supper and angry because he was wet to the skin. She sent him to his bedroom to change into dry clothes and David heard her in the kitchen, singing to herself an old Jewish song about a man going home to the house he had lived in as a boy and finding everything strange, and no one who remembered him.

When his father came home, David saw he was troubled. He did not say *"Shalom,"* nor did he kiss the *mezzuzah* on the doorjamb when he came through the doorway. His mother too knew immediately, and said in Yiddish: "What is, Jakob?"

"Nothing, Leah, nothing."

"Tell me what is, Jakob. I know something goes badly."

"Ach! It is the old man from downstairs. My heart is twisted for him," his father said, taking his wet coat off slowly, and heavily, and hanging it on the open closet door to dry. "The boarder, the dark one, has led away his daughter."

"She is?"

"What else? Yuh."

"I should go down. . . ."

"No, Leah, it is not our business. We should not mix in." And after a moment. "The old one makes them married."

"That is not wise. She is so young, too young."

"Sure. Of course it is not wise," his father said, suddenly, and, it seemed to David, unreasonably angry. "And what else should he do? He should make them a party?"

"He should maybe help the girl to—"

"Ssha! The small one doesn't understand."

And David knew they were talking deliberately so that he could not understand, and he hated it. Although he did not understand, he said aloud, "I do so understand," but when his parents coaxed him to say more, to say what he understood, he would stubbornly say no more.

He sat in his bedroom alone for a long time, not able to hear what his parents were saying, but from the rise and fall of their voices, he knew they were talking about the Vecchiones. One sentence floated into his room in his father's voice. "We should not mix ourselves in." Downstairs, there were strange noises from the open windows, shouting and crying and heavy falling noises like furniture being moved. Out on the *bocci* field the old men came like shadows, gathered in little knots under the night lights, their brown hands flying, their heads turned toward the Vecchiones' house, and then went away without rolling the little black balls and turned out the night lights.

Later, when the light in his parents' room went out, in his pajamas David sneaked downstairs. Quietly he scratched at the Vecchiones' door, and there was a sudden silence, then a whispering, before the door was opened a crack and Joe's thin, dark face looked out.

"It's me, David."

For a moment Joe stood there, looking at him as though he was a stranger. "Go back upstairs," he said finally, in a slow, choked voice.

David opened his mouth to speak but Joe was suddenly seeing

him, recognizing him, mussing his hair and saying: "It's got nothing to do with you, David. You're still our little friend. Now, go back to bed." He gave his face a slight pat on the cheek. "Go on, there isn't anything you can do," Joe said, and then softly closed the door. David stole back upstairs to his bedroom, wondering how to get to Pop and tell him what he felt and how he wanted to help.

In the middle of the night, he awoke suddenly, feeling feverishly hot and unaware that noises had awakened him until he heard sounds like the faraway chopping of trees. At the open window, he saw Pop Vecchione out in the fields, bent double, head down, with a hoe in his hands, furiously beating another row of his tomatoes into bloody splotches on the moon-pale earth. David wanted to shout to him, call out his comfort, assure Pop that everything would be all right, just as it used to be. As he watched the hoe flash in the moonlight, he wished he could sing out—something, anything!— loud and clear and strong, like a pulse up toward the blind eyes of the stars and down to the small jackknifed figure of the old man. He remembered the music they had listened to, the music the old man had taught him about, and the sounds of the aria from the *Pearl Fishers* went singing themselves through his head. But now the aria was filled with torn and broken sounds as if it was being sobbed, not sung. Strangely, in his mind, it seemed less like the smooth Italian sadness of the aria and more like the bitter Hebraic mourning of *"Eli, Eli . . .* God, O God, why hast thou forsaken me?" And then he knew that no song would help, nothing he could do for or say to Pop Vecchione would help. He heard his father's running footsteps behind and felt his deep breathing and sleep-warm figure at his back, but he could not turn to him and speak.

So he stood staring out at the old man and the *bocci* alley, the strange tangle of the *Pearl Fishers* and "Eli, Eli" a dark flame in his mind and a bitterness in his mouth and throat until he saw his father, looking like a scarecrow in his flapping bathrobe and white skullcap, climbing the backyard picket fence and running across the furrowed field to the old man. When he got there, David saw him take the hoe from Pop's hands and throw it to the ground. Then he began to help the old man across the field almost back to the house. Together they went over the fence, his father almost lifting the old man over the pickets, and finally, when they were beneath the window, in the darkness of the stairwell, David heard the crushed crying of the old man and his father's "Sssha" sounding as it had when as a child he had awakened from a nightmare and his father had come to comfort him.

And in the new silence of the night, he was frightened, cold, and trembling. Beneath the twisted peach trees the black *bocci* balls looked strange and ominous, and the tomatoes on the ground were spattered blood. He felt someone behind him, and when he turned, his father was there, smiling down and patting his shoulder.

"The old man, Pop, is all right now. And Toni will be too, maybe," his father said quietly. "Come to bed now, my son. There is nothing more to be done."

David got into bed and covered himself, aware that his father had called the Vecchiones by their first names for the first time, names David hadn't even known his father knew because his father had always called them "they." In the doorway his father stopped and looked back and David could not see his face clearly in the darkness, but he could hear his words plainly: "It will be very hard for them. We will do what we can." Then, with the warmth and gratitude for his father in him sudden and intense as pain, David heard the sharp closing of his door and the silence of the night thickened and the night went slowly back to sleep.

Roman Portrait

In the bed nearest the door in Ward Seven Marguerite Brooks saw him first, while he was still unconscious, lying lumplike beneath the gray blankets stenciled U.S. ARMY. Only one eye and an eyebrow were exposed above the bandages covering the lower part of his face: all the rest of his head was bandaged except for a little triangle of flesh under the one eye that wrinkled pale yellow against the white gauze. From the window behind his head, bars of sunshine and shadow fell across the folded white sheet and gray blankets that covered him, blankets that sagged and fell away from his right hip where there had been a leg. The little white identification card at the bed was neatly typewritten, but at first she felt nausea and her age and could not focus on it. When she did, it read, "Second Lieu-tenant Willis Burton," and then his serial number, his outfit—an Air Force fighter squadron—and before she could read further, one of the boys in one of the other beds called, "Say Marguerite, what have you got today?"

It was Mark Terman, the infantry captain. She looked away from Lt. Burton's bedtag and went to Mark's bed, hearing herself say casually, "Some cigarettes, American this time, and some Italian candies."

Mark rolled over and called to the three others still in the six-bed ward: "All right, guys, rise and shine. Your favorite gray lady is here."

As she gave each of the men two packs of cigarettes and several Italian *torrones,* she felt gray, but not much like a lady. "Good morning, cheerful,'' Jim Brower, a black-haired giant artilleryman greeted her. "Don't I get a kiss from my favorite Red Cross gal?"

Marguerite smiled and bent to kiss his dark, pain-ridden face. "Now why don't you shave, Jim, before you ask a lady to kiss you?" she grimaced wryly. "Did you kiss your girl like that at home?" But she couldn't concentrate on the usual banter. Although these were also recovering from serious wounds, they would be whole and look like normal people, but Major Ames had told her that morning that Willis Burton would not only be missing a right leg, but even with plastic surgery there wouldn't be much hope for reconstructing his face. Burton had crashed in flames on a routine strafing mission, hit by heavy machine gun fire from the ground. He'd been badly burned, leg and face worst of all. The Germans, retreating, had left him behind without first aid, and when the infantry had picked him up, Burton was wandering around near a German aid station, blind and groping. After stops at a few hospitals, they'd sent him back to Rome as fast as they could.

Now he was here in her ward. She'd never before had an amputation: how would he act? was he married? what had he looked like before? how about his mother? Marguerite thought about his mother for a moment before she realized that she was thinking of Kirk shot down over Germany, two years ago—"We are sorry to inform you, your son Lt. Kirk Brooks . . . missing in action"—and still no news. In the round of war and work and wounded she had not thought of him in many months.

When Marguerite had gone through the other wards, given out the cigarettes and *torrones,* written a letter for the little Clark boy in Ward Eleven, and read a story to the glowering blind Bernstein in Ward Nine, she went back to her own quarters. Her forty-eight years seemed suddenly a burden she carried on her shoulders as if by a dogged, bent-head pack animal. She felt she needed a rest. Perhaps it was only the Roman spring. Maybe malaria. They said spring brought out a lot of malaria in Rome. Well, she'd take a check tomorrow. Then, in the little yellow-walled room, she laughed aloud. It was the first time in a long time that she'd thought of herself in that finicky way. There simply wasn't enough time here, and now, with even more to do, she was acting as she'd acted when she was still a matron in Newton and concerned with bridge parties, the community chest, and her latest hairdo.

That evening, hesitating at the door to Ward Seven, Marguerite heard the broken groaning of Lt. Burton. Major Ames was sitting next to him and she stood at the foot of the bed while the boy—it seemed absurd to call him Lieutenant, as if the Army could force a boy into manhood by the magic of a word—squirmed beneath the blankets. The lower part of his face, naked beneath the bandage, was twisted into a downward curve of pain and his mouth bubbled little groans. "My leg, my leg. God, my leg."

The Major did not say hello but motioned her to follow him out into the hall. "He's pretty bad off," Major Ames said. "I've been talking to him since he came to." He fingered his stethoscope absently with long nicotine-stained fingers. "He's so damned young it'll be harder for him than the others. The leg and the eye would have been more than enough, but the face . . . . "

"Bad, Major?"

"Pretty bad. If it'd been treated right off, it would still be rotten. But it wasn't. We'll do skin grafts, but it won't be pretty."

"Anything I can do?" Marguerite asked tentatively.

Major Ames looked at her, his young face gray-lined, his brown hair whitening back in streaks from the forehead as if it too had gone sleepless. He laughed mirthlessly. "Sure, a new leg or face or . . . . " He stopped and took a crumpled packet of cigarettes from his pocket. Empty. When Marguerite gave him a fresh pack from her box, he ripped it open impatiently and lit a cigarette, the match fluttering in his shaking hands. "I'm sorry," he said. "That was dumb. I'm getting bad myself. Probably fluff out one of these days and get myself a Section Eight." He drew deeply on the cigarette and blew tight smoke circles from his pursed lips. "There is something you really *can* do. His other eye is okay—thank God—but he's got to be able to take it about the face and the leg. That'll be tough."

"You mean cheer him up?" Marguerite asked, not believing anyone could ask that of her.

"Something like that, but more so. If he loses hope, he'll go nuts," the Major said. "He's got to believe in tomorrow, and the day after. He's got to have a hope for himself, a faith, maybe just a belief in the future. I don't really know what."

A faith? A hope for the future? Did anyone have a hope for the future? She had always told herself she kept going because Kirk was coming back. That was her special future, Kirk coming back and making her a mother, with a family, again, with the old house in Newton overlooking the Charles River filled with Kirk and a wife he would choose and children she could help look after. Without Kirk, she was only another widow, lost, childless, without a tomorrow.

"You'll try, Marguerite?" Major Ames said. He took her arm. "There's no one I'd rather try with that kid than you."

"Thanks," she said ironically.

"I mean it," he replied. "The nurses are overworked. You Red Crossers are busy and we don't have a psychiatrist around. Except me." He grinned wearily. "And I'm really only a very mediocre surgeon, nothing more."

When she went back into the ward, the boy was still, his long, big-knuckled hands clutching the blanket, white tendons tight outlines in the pale flesh. The triangle around his good eye became alive and the eyebrow seemed to bristle, while beneath it the coal-furnace eye blazed with anguish. As the eye fixed on her, she could feel the dark iris and pupil merge into a single darkness trying to cut her out of his sight. "Hello, Lt. Burton," she said softly (again the absurd title), "I'm Marguerite Brooks, the gray lady here."

Burton said nothing, but the yellow lid blinked over the coal-furnace black of the eye. A single tear overlapped at the corner and trickled into the white gauze. He turned his bandaged head away from her on the pillow and she heard his quiet fractured crying. To the others she gave out cigarettes and some new magazines from the States, but she couldn't bring herself to stay and talk. Even the usually cheerful Jim Brower was quiet, and Mark Terman wouldn't meet her eyes. They all lay stiffly in bed, listening to the boy's crying.

Late that night, the O.D. came to her room and woke her. "Mrs. Brooks," he shook her gently. "Mrs. Brooks. Major Ames wants you over at Ward Seven right away."

Instantly she was awake, but she couldn't shake off her dream of Kirk. Both of them were flying in an airplane over the Charles River with the buildings of Boston looking beautiful and cleansed in the sun. As the sun tottered behind the horizon, rivers of darkness ran wildly between the golden buildings in the streets below. "Yes, yes," she said unclearly. "I'll be right there."

"Sure you're awake?" the O.D. asked.

"Of course I'm awake!" she said, unreasonably irritated. "I'll be there in a couple of minutes."

She dressed quickly, fumbling with straps and buttons. Splashing a little cold water on her face, she thought suddenly: "It's for Burton. My God!" She tried to remember her dream again—so long since she'd dreamt of Kirk—but the cold water had shocked it out of her. All she could remember was something about her and Kirk—or was it Lt. Burton?—riding in a long sloop in the dark rivers of Rome.

At Ward Seven she hesitated, as always before entering, and she heard Major Ames saying, "Just tell us what you're talking about. We'll help you get it. Or we'll get it for you. But you've got to help us, or we can't help you." He stopped and turned at the sound of her step, his young-old face sagging, as if, for a moment, the bones beneath had broken and the flesh collapsed. Marguerite nodded, watching the triangle of eye and brow in the swathe of white gauze. The gauze itself looked darkened in the yellow light sprawling on the ward floor from the tiny bulb in the corridor. The black-haired eyebrow was strangely arched and the simmering eye beneath opened and stared at her.

She turned to the Major. "Better get some sleep. You've got an operation in—" she looked at the sickly green luminous hands on her wristwatch—"just about three hours."

The Major stood up and lit a cigarette. They walked into the corridor but it was a moment before he seemed to get a second wind to talk with. "Hysterical all night. Screaming, groaning, crying, and whatnot. Yelling about some picture. Christ only knows what kind of picture, or where?''

"His mother? Girl?"

Major Ames shrugged. "Don't know. Wouldn't tell *me* anything. Just 'my picture, my picture,' like his life depended on it.''

"Maybe it's his wife and children.''

"Young for kids. Maybe a wife, I don't know. Records haven't caught up with him yet.'' One hand went up through his graying hair and he saw his watch. "I'll be a wreck for surgery. See what you can do for him, Marg.''

"I'll try.''

"Good enough,'' the Major said. He turned and walked down the corridor, leaving his shadow thinning and elongating on the floor behind him.

Marguerite went back into the ward, sat down in the cane bottom chair next to the bed and took the tense hand that lay on the blankets between her own two palms. She could feel the chill even through the callous and where her fingers curved around his wrist, the faint beat of the blood inside. Slowly she warmed his hand with her own, saying nothing, taking first one hand and then the other between her own warm hands and chafing them.

Then Burton began to speak. Quietly, with a voice that had more breath than timbre, he said: "Listen. I don't know why but I know I can trust you.'' His breath was a sharp hissing. "I had leave in Rome and I was having a big time. I was flying a lot before then, maybe even a little flak-happy from it, but I had money in my pocket and a couple days and I wanted to make it rich. One night we all got a little tight and George—he was my buddy, shot down a couple days before I was—got an idea about getting his picture painted. Said he was tired of snapshots. I said sure, sure, you know the way a guy will when he's tight and everything's smooth.'' His hand fell on the flat empty space below his thigh.

"Next day we were sober, but George found a little place that had this Eyetie portrait painter, took me along just for the laughs. The Eyetie said he was a big shot before the war but he was in a little room and after we bargained for a while he said he'd paint George.

But George got cold feet, something about getting jinxed if you got painted, a kind of voodoo he picked up somewhere. I saw some of the other paintings in the room and decided I'd go ahead. I hadn't really expected to, but it seemed like a good idea. And like I said, I had a roll and I was feeling no pain. So I came for a little bit every day while I was in Rome and he painted me.''

For a moment, he was quiet, breathing thickly and heavily. ''I wrote my mother about it, told her I'd send it to her—a full-size picture—and she's expecting it. I know she is.'' The hands on the blanket became fists. ''I'VE GOT TO GET IT,'' he shouted suddenly, his voice hoarse and cracking.

''Sure you've got to,'' Marguerite said soothingly. ''I'll help you. We'll get it together. Don't you worry now.'' She held his hand tightly and it reminded her somehow of Kirk and the crazy way he'd cried about a blue flannel elephant he'd used to take to sleep with him every night. When it had gotten so filthy that she couldn't bear to have him touch it, she'd thrown it out and Kirk had cried and cried until she'd had to hunt through half of Boston before she found another blue flannel elephant like it. Then Kirk had taken it happily into his bed and cried himself to sleep because he had it back. The blood beating in Burton's wrists was almost like the beat of Kirk's sobbing when she'd held him against her and promised him his blue elephant.

''When my leave was up,'' Burton said after a while, ''Angelo, the Eyetie painter, said it was okay. He could finish it up without me and I could come back for it. I was going to fly down for it in about a month, but then . . . . '' His voice trailed off into breathlessness and Marguerite felt the trembling become a shaking inside him, like a braked airplane engine roaring and shaking.

''What was his name?'' she asked, more to distract him than for the information. ''His second name.''

''I don't know. You know we never ask Eyeties for their second names.''

She tried to find out the street name and, failing that, what the painter looked like, but Burton couldn't describe his Angelo. He seemed embarrassed when she asked until she understood that he had probably been drunk every time he went there. ''Tell me where you were staying and how you got there," she said, the idea seeming so simple that it was odd it had not occurred to her before. "If you can remember that, I'll follow the same route."

Burton smiled for the first time. "That's a good idea," he said. Although he couldn't remember exactly, nor did he know any of the street names, he gave her left and right turns and approximate distances in blocks and she wrote it down. From what he said, Marguerite thought it was probably a few blocks off the Corso, between it and the Via di Ripetta, but she couldn't be sure. In the morning she would try her luck. For a moment, taken with the scheme, she did not hear Burton begin to whimper, "I've got to have it, Missis Brooks. I got to send it home before they send me," he said and broke into inarticulate crying. Again Marguerite remembered Kirk crying broken-heartedly about the blue flannel elephant, his face tight with pleading. As though it were perfectly natural, she began to sing Kirk's favorite song in a low voice as she had always done to comfort Kirk, and again she took Burton's hands in hers.

> The minstrel boy to the war has gone,
> In the ranks of death you'll find him.
> His father's sword he hath girded on
> And his wild harp slung behind him. . . .

She sang quietly, hoping that the others were not disturbed, yet knowing by the irregular sounds of their breathing that they were all awake and listening. She sang the song over and over again until the hands in hers relaxed and fell limp and Burton's breathing became quietly regular. Then, wearily, she went back to bed.

In the morning, in the hospital mess, she met Major Ames. They faced each other over the green oilclothed wooden table and she had to have a full cup of black coffee before she could say, faintly, "He's looking for a portrait of himself before he crashed."

The Major's cup stopped on the way to his mouth, wavered, then continued to his lips. "Christ!" he said in the pause.

"I'm going to try to locate it for him," she said after she told him Burton's story.

"That's not much to go on."

"That's all we've got."

The Major smiled. "Sometimes, Marg, I think you should have been a surgeon."

"That I couldn't do," she said, forcing a grin. "But somehow I'll find that painting." She felt her voice tightening in her throat and sticking there until she washed it back down with the hot, bitter coffee.

The Major looked at her uneasily. "Don't get yourself too tied up in this thing."

"Yes," she said. "I know."

In the afternoon she got a jeep and a map of Rome from the transportation depot and made her plan, outlining the whole area she had to cover. That was on Monday. All that day, she tried, walking through the dirty back alleys, asking the bare-breasted women nursing their children on the steps, asking the little boys soliciting for their sisters who tried to sell her fountain pens and religious ornaments, asking the dying old men smoking their stained pipes if they knew a painter named Angelo. None did. Or if they did, no one would tell her.

At the hospital there was a note on her bureau asking her to go to Ward Seven. Major Ames was waiting in the corridor outside. "He got violent. Been yelling we were keeping his painting from him because we didn't want to let him get his leg back from it. He tried to get out of bed a couple of times and almost fell out so I had to give him some morphine. That'll carry him through the night anyway. Give you a night's sleep too," he added, smiling. Then, seriously, "Find the painting?"

She shook her head.

"Keep trying. Let the rest go, and work on that. He's getting worse about it."

"I'll keep looking," she said, turning away.

It was the same all week and it seemed to her that nobody in all Rome had ever heard of Angelo the portrait painter. Perhaps there was no such man and it was all Lt. Burton's fevered imagination. But every day she searched, a little more desperately, because she knew that the Major was keeping Burton under sedatives to keep him from blowing his top. At the end of the second week, the O.D.

woke her in the middle of the night again. She ran to Ward Seven in her robe, her pajamas flapping beneath. Burton had come out of the morphine screaming. As she got there, she heard Mark Terman shout: "If you don't shut him up, he'll drive us all nuts. Shut him up or get him the hell out of here."

"He'll be all right," Marguerite said, "and so will you."

"He's tough to take with yelling about that picture," Jim Brower said.

"Get some sleep, all of you. I'll look after Lt. Burton," she said, deliberately using his title. The night nurse nodded to her and whispered that Burton was going to get another hypo.

"It's in an alley, Miss Brooks," Burton whispered raucously, "a dirty alley with little pools and water dripping from the stones of the houses. There're little fire escapes with clotheslines hung from them. Angelo's there with my painting. Angelo's *there,* he's *there,* I know he is."

"Sssh! Of course he's there and I'm going to see him tomorrow and get it for you."

"Are you?" he asked innocently. "Thank God. It's the only thing that can help me. I've got to have it. My painting."

The nurse came back and rolled up his pajama sleeve. As the needle bit into the flesh of his arm, Burton's hand gripped hers hard, holding her fingers as though she were the last solid thing in the world. Slowly, slowly, his fingers went lax and Marguerite went back to her room.

That night she dreamed of Kirk again and this time the three of them, Kirk, Burton, and she, were riding a squashy blue elephant through a long, cracked mirror into dark alleys where lines of dirty wash were strung from house to house, dripping water into pools of blood on cobbled streets. In the morning she was still tired but when Major Ames told her she would have to get the painting quick if it was going to do Burton any good, she couldn't swallow her breakfast coffee. "You look haggard," he said. "Maybe you better let it go."

"No!" She found she had shouted and forced her voice down to normal. "Not yet. A few more days. I've just got to find that painting."

"You're too involved, Marg," the Major said, and when she didn't answer him he sat silently staring at her for a long while. Then he got up and left.

In the late afternoon of the third week of search, Marguerite found Angelo the portrait painter in a tiny, filthy street only a little way off the Corso. The fire escapes turned out to be balconies that almost touched across the narrow street. Lines of battered clothes hung limp in the spring heat. Two boys wrestled on the littered cobblestones while a third, his back turned, urinated against the wall of a house. Angelo's place was on the second floor. The little boy in the street that she had asked about Angelo turned out to be Vittorio, Angelo's nephew, who spoke a little English and was Angelo's solicitor among the English and American troops. She had heard him in the street saying loudly to a British Tommy: "Pitcha painted. Putty good pitcha. Cheap. . . . " And Marguerite knew she had found Angelo, so she followed the boy to where he was urinating against the wall and told him that she wanted to see Angelo.

He took her into the alleyway, through a side entrance, and up two flights of narrow, winding stairs that led to Angelo's room. Angelo was painting an old woman in a shapeless brown dress, sitting on a box near the open window. He was a little man with no hair and a large aquiline Roman nose. The little Vittorio told him that the American lady comes for the Lt. Burton's portrait. Angelo bowed to Marguerite, still holding palette and brushes, and yet managing to seem perfectly natural. "That is the very young one, no?" he asked.

She nodded.

"He is not— ," the painter asked gravely.

"No, but he is wounded severely, deprived of a leg and of the sight of one eye," she replied.

The painter's fine old head and nose bent toward the floor, his bald spot looking almost as if it had been deliberately tonsured. "The horror," he whispered, " . . . and the stupidity."

The painter seemed suddenly to remind himself and sent Vittorio for the portrait. It was wrapped and the boy dragged it back because it was too big for him to carry. Marguerite took it and extended the roll of *lire* she had in her pocketbook. Gently he shook his head. "The Lieutenant has already paid," he said gravely. "More than the price."

After Angelo had said goodbye and bowed her out, she gave the money to Vittorio for his uncle. The boy thanked her profusely and helped her get the painting into the jeep. Not until she had driven back onto the Corso did she remember with a queer inner quaver the quiet, unmoving hopelessness of the woman Angelo had been painting. The woman had not moved nor had her face changed its expression during her stay in the room. But suddenly the triumph of the portrait found overwhelmed her. She forgot the stonelike woman and her own uneasiness about Lt. Burton when he saw the painting.

Back at the hospital at twilight Marguerite struggled with the painting until she got to the hospital door, where she met Major Ames coming out. His tired gray face changed in a moment to a youthful brightness. "You found it!" he exulted.

"Sure. Pitcha painted. Putty good pitcha. Cheap," Marguerite mimicked Vittorio.

"You look at it?"

"No," she said. "I wanted him to see it first."

The Major took the painting from her, carrying it easily. When they got to Ward Seven, the Major waited in the corridor. She found Burton lying quietly in his bed, the twilight blue-gray as smoke in the room, the lights still unlit. In the little triangle of flesh and brow in the bandage Burton's eye opened and stared. He smiled weakly.

She felt inadequate and suddenly tired as he began to shout, "You found it! You found it!" trying to push himself up on his elbows and falling back on the pillow panting with effort, and she had the same strange sense of foreboding, almost of despair, that had surrounded the stonelike woman Angelo had been painting. "Bring it in, Major," she called, trying to sound cheerful and triumphant.

The Major brought it in, leaned it against a chair, and began to unwrap it. The room grew darker as he tore impatiently at the flimsy cords that held the paper, and then he tore the paper off into a crumpled heap on the floor.

"I can't see it," Burton cried.

"I'll put the lights on," the Major said. He went into the corridor.

"And I'll hold it up so you can see it better," Marguerite said, putting her arm about his shoulders and propping him up to a sitting position.

The lights flickered on and streamed down on the portrait of a slim young aviator, bareheaded and erect, looking out of the window in Angelo's room, the flight wings silvery on his olive drab tunic, the rows of ribbons neatly underlining them. The face was incredibly young looking, open and searching, with eyes dark as polished berries, eyes that seemed to look beyond the man, beyond the painter, beyond tomorrow. He stood tall and firm on two legs in sharply creased and spotless pinks. It was an athletic figure, looking strange without motion, almost as if it were going to leap immediately into action, spring out of Angelo's window, or off the canvas into the ward. Behind her she could feel the others in the ward straining to see the painting, and holding Burton erect she could feel his own straining forward. She found herself staring at the painting, finding it combining with a memory of Kirk running for a football, catching a touchdown pass the last time she had seen him play at college.

She tried to pull herself back because she felt she was sinking into the painting, tried to make herself criticize it—see how Angelo had caught all the lights in the dark hair—as she would any painting. It was a good portrait in thick, colorful oils. She could tell it was good by the eyes, the dark smolder of them and the craggy eyebrows. It was Lt. Burton all right. No. It *had been* Lt. Burton. The same strange thing shook inside her and then Burton turned his body to hers, his one eye staring wildly out of the bandages, and threw his arms around her, sobbing.

And as she felt his body against her bosom, Marguerite thought again of Kirk, his blue elephant and his high slim twisting for that forward pass, and finally of the stonelike impassiveness of the old woman model at Angelo's. In the portrait Marguerite knew that the boy had found what he wanted, and didn't want, and she too had found something of Kirk and his youth, and had lost something she had loved and clung to for years since that telegram. Behind her she

heard the others lie back, the beds sighing with their weight. Someone struck a match and she heard Mark Terman mutter: "Well,
that's that." Burton's sobbing tore something into motion inside
her, some worn stoniness that shook apart with his trembling, like
rocks cracking, and she sat by the bed, her head face down on
Burton's sheets.

The Dürer Hands

When Douglas Longstreth walked out of the bar, quickly past the
newspaper and cigar stand, and across the small hotel foyer toward
the telephone booths, he did not see her standing before the elevators. But when the boy opened the elevator doors, and in that spe-
cially acquired two lines of refined English grafted on Ninth Avenue
New Yorkese said, "Ground floor, please. Watch your step getting
off," it turned his head automatically. He knew he should be surprised, and perhaps even deeply moved, but he wasn't: he looked at
her only with that faint curiosity and detachment that was now his
for all seeing, and thought: "Fifteen years and she hasn't changed."
The same dark face was set in a concentration that he and others had
often mistaken for a frown, and the same dark-blonde hair had the
look of deliberately ordered disarray. "A sweet disorder . . . " he
thought, and smiled or grimaced, he didn't know which, because he
caught the flicker of his face unawares in the long panel of mirror set
between the elevators and was unable to finish the quotation. The
body seemed the same, although he knew you couldn't tell, at least
not with clothes on: the legs long, the head held almost skeptically to
one side, and the stride as she went by the elevator boy, whose cor-
nered eyes fluttered quickly up and down her, was the slightly unco-
ordinated walk that had always reminded him of an adolescent girl
newly, and not quite well, acquainted with her sex.

Fifteen years, he thought, and it didn't seem to make much difference, but why then should he have remembered the exact number?

"Margaret," he called almost inaudibly, then louder as the elevator boy made the clacking ritual of preparing to close the doors. She looked back, turning only her head, and seeing him for a moment was undecided; then, still moving, her whole body wheeled back toward him, the white, good-morning smile came up like surf, and she was saying, "Douglas! Douglas!" speaking his name like a talisman. She hurried to him—the elevator closed polished brass doors behind her—and held out her hands. When he took them, the suede gloves were like some softer, turned-out inner skin, a warmer animal flesh.

Together they laughed, saying in unison: "It's fifteen years!"

Margaret was looking at him and over her shoulder in the mirror he saw how he had changed: the thickness, almost the grossness, that even good tailoring couldn't hide. Well, I'm forty-five, he thought, that's middle-aged. Why expect more? Should the body still be lean, the face unlined, the hair thick and black? He knew she would remember the other body, combat-slender and hospital-pale, but it was another spirit she would miss, one he'd long since lost.

"We still have that simultaneity," he said, shuddering with a sudden chill, then knowing he couldn't willingly have chosen a worse sentence.

Something leaped beneath her face and Douglas saw its age and difference but the familiarity held him and masked its strangeness. "Oh, I don't know," she said too casually, "it's a natural enough thing to say."

"Natural?"

"Well," she seemed to relent, though from what he wasn't sure, "it's the first thing you'd think of—how long ago it was—if you walk right smack into Douglas Longstreth in a hotel lobby. Are you staying here?"

"Yes. Are you?"

She nodded, laughing again, but this time he was sure something was different, very different, but just what he couldn't put his finger on.

In the winter of 1944 the war was not quite over for everyone, but it was for him. A mortar fragment through the ribs had severed his right kidney, simple and undramatic, and that was it. It wasn't the million-dollar one perhaps, but he didn't really care: he wanted only to get out of the war, out of the Army, and besides, he told himself, the whole show was pretty much over by then anyway. He worried about having one kidney and had nightmares of all his waste spilling abruptly into the hollow of his body like some inward venom to poison him, and sometimes, morbidly, he wondered what had happened to the kidney there in the surgeon's tent in France, and hoped that it had not merely been thrown to some dog, but had at least been buried, though what difference that made he couldn't reasonably see.

After ten days at home, trying to make small talk with his father and his father's new wife, their asking him daily about "his plans" and his onetime boss calling half-a-dozen times to say that his old job was waiting for him and that they needed engineers badly, Douglas came back to New York. He took an apartment in the Village, registered for some engineering courses at N.Y.U. that he never went to, and lived quietly on the G.I. Bill which, sardonically, he told himself should be called "52-20 or fight!" He knew almost no one, spoke to almost no one, but there was a cry in him that wouldn't let him sleep nights, that kept him stalking the streets like some nighttime animal. He'd been wounded at night, he reminded himself, hoping that the recognition would exorcise it and it would go away, but it didn't.

One such night, walking down Horatio Street—that he remembered the street was rare because all the Village streets seemed the same then—he looked up at the blue and white street sign and thought, "There are more things in heaven and earth, Horatio, than are dreamt of in your philosophy," and as he thought it, bemused by how pompous it sounded, he saw the dogs. A black speckled bull and a white and tan terrier, they circled each other like old gladiators or tired wrestlers, who knew that sooner or later one would leave the other an opening, a place to thrust, a limb to pin a hold on, to pierce a heart, or break an arm. It was a kind of war too, and still a game, the way war had been—"Goddam it Longstreth, draw some fire there!"—and he watched the sniffling circling weaving of the dogs with an old unremembered joy.

She was leaning against the whitewashed brick wall across the street, staring at the dogs with a fascination that was horror, her white mouth gaping, two childlike fingers laid to her lips, her eyes fixed, and for an instant he wanted, strangely, to slap the look from her face. The sound of his voice carrying across the narrow, alleylike street and echoing back was the first he'd spoken to her. "A lot like people," he said, "aren't they?"

"No," she answered hoarsely, her lips almost unmoving, "people are a lot like them."

She watched the dogs and he watched her until, when with a strangling gargle she swiveled to the wall, he knew without looking that the bull had mounted. He walked across to her, took her chin in the hollow of his hand, and turned her face to him. Her eyes were closed, and behind the long violet-shadowed lids the eyeballs raced like scattered pebbles, and when her eyes opened it was like a room where drawn blinds suddenly had their angle tilted and slashed the walls with light, and inside him something turned like a doorknob. Her jaw rested tense as knotted rope in his palm; he let his hand fall, sliding down her neck, over her shoulder, along her arm, until he held her by the elbow and led her away through the street darkness, feeling the knot in her loosen beside him into a flutter, a quailing tremor, then a spasm of sobs. He walked her through the streets as if he were sobering a drunk, measuring his stride to hers, until the shaking stilled: then he took her to his place.

He fought taking her there, mustering his resolve like clenched fists, but all his walking only took them back there each time. She followed him up the three flights of stairs like a child; when he looked back, her eyes were on the backs of his shoes. Just before his landing, he turned, took her chin in his hands again, hating to bring anyone into those rooms he had fortified—against the world, the war, women, and his wounds, perhaps even against himself—and felt his hands then close around her throat, the arteries like wind-driven stems beating against his palms.

"How do you know," he asked deliberately, "that I won't take you up there— " his head inclined toward the door "—and kill you? Or rob you?"

"Kill me? Rob me?" she said, her upper lip ironically arching, her blue eyes sky-open and candid. "Of what? What more could *you* do?"

"Much more," he said leadenly. "I could kill your body."

"Is that so important?"

"Most important."

She put her warm palms over his cold hands and pressed them against her throat, "If you think that, I don't suppose you will."

At the door she asked, "Are you a soldier?" She was looking at his khakis and combat boots.

"I was."

Her eyebrows asked the question and he had to laugh. "No, I'm not a deserter, or at least not in the sense you mean. Not even A.W.O.L. Nothing so romantic, or *Farewell-to-Arms* like. It's much more permanent. I was wounded."

"I'm sorry," she murmured.

"I'm still alive, why be sorry?"

"Because being dead's not bad, it's being wounded that hurts."

In war and in life it was a point he thought she was too young and too far from death to make, and surely one he was not prepared to debate. He shrugged and turned the key in the lock. "Okay," he breathed, "come on in."

Douglas had invited her to dinner and Margaret had promised to call as soon as she knew she was free. She'd hesitated when he proposed it, but he could not bear to beg her, nor plead with "For old times' sake," which came unbidden to his lips, sensing that if he did it would be destroyed, but just what *it* was, he didn't know either.

Though he hated hotel rooms, even expense-account suites like this one, Douglas found himself waiting there, looking out the window at Central Park, wondering when she would call. Call or not, he told himself, it didn't matter. That was over; he had finished it fifteen years ago. He'd packed it in then, yet the detachment he had since bought and paid for so dearly with his marriage to Caroline, his children, and his divorce seemed to be paying out of his hands like reel torn by a leaping fish. He'd made his share of messes, more of them he supposed than most, but being sorry wasn't enough: you had to say "No more!" and mean it, mean it in a way that permanently cut you off from making more messes.

Almost automatically he pressed his flattened palm against his back where once his kidney had pulsed beneath, and then, aware that he was doing it and feeling only the puckered ridge of scar tissue across his ribs, pulled his hands away. "You always do that," Caroline had said to him at the end, in a relief of viciousness, "when you're acting as if you can still feel, when you want to give someone the impression that you've got an unhealed wound hurting you. Or when you're playing wounded by life."

And when he had twisted in pain, his hand once more searching out the back of his rib cage, and remembered acidly that woman was Adam's rib, she had given him her *coup de grace:* "You give me a pain. You think you're sensitive, but you just confuse irascibility with sensitivity. They might just as well have killed you in the war, because as far as I'm concerned, you've got nothing left here," she tapped her still lovely breast, "except some small piece of electronic equipment that deludes you into imagining you're alive. As far as you're concerned, and even if you don't know it yet, you're dead."

He didn't hear the knock at the door, but when it came again, Douglas opened the door irritably and found Margaret there, smiling. "Come in," he invited awkwardly, "I didn't expect you. I thought we'd meet in the lobby."

"Don't tell me you've changed that much, Douglas," she said, laughing, and walked past him. "Besides, it's not the first time I've come to your rooms now is it?"

Her casual reminder pained him and the smell of her perfume—it was *Cuir de Russie,* and they had their private jokes about what it *really* meant—made him remember the brown berry beauty mark she carried beneath her right breast. He had always touched it, lovingly, wonderingly, hopefully, in a way as if somehow it would make everything beneath turn out—not the way he gripped his back.

"Nor I to yours," he said, only half trying to hurt her back.

She shared an apartment with two other girls then, with rooms all strangely shaped trapezoid cubes except for a rectangular bathroom, so that he always felt everything—the people, the talk, the world—was askew there, nothing in line, nothing plumb, nothing level. Only much later had he realized how much he hated that apartment, its disorder, its broken venetian blinds, its unframed posters from the *plazas de toros* of Spain and the Mediterranean resorts of France—Villefranche, Nice, St. Tropez, Juan-les-Pins— and the African sculpture that was Margaret's mania: small twisted fertility statues in black and brown woods that made all sex a somber, rough-hewn rutting.

And the people, the constant coming and going of theater people—she thought she wanted to be a stage designer—cold blonde actresses, pansy leading men, drunken character actors, and slick directors and agents on the make, their perpetual talk loud, loud even over the phonograph always turned on and always blaring show tunes, so that everyone else could and would hear their emptiness.

In the abrupt way Margaret had when she was sorry, she apologized. "I didn't mean to embarrass you," she said.

Because she had embarrassed him, Douglas silently reprimanded himself for behaving like a callow boy and to keep his hands busy went about making drinks while she stood at the window, looking down at the park and asking questions. He was surprised at how quickly and simply he could sum up fifteen years; it had not been that quick or simple in the days, but now a few sentences covered the years. He was vice-president of an electronics firm, in New York on business. He was divorced; their mother had their two sons; and he did a lot of traveling now. As he told it, he didn't know which was the greater boasting, the successes or the failures; he wasn't even sure he knew which were which.

The secret thing leaped beneath her face again while they drank, and he remembered how her eyes glazed like blue china when she'd been drinking, how her mouth flowed soft and wanton, and how sometimes, unaccountably, she could drink like a fish, and other times one drink made her sick.

She told him she was married to a lawyer, Mitchell Wilkinson, had two daughters and a son, and was in New York to go shopping. Her husband had gone to Ipswich to see a client and would meet her later in the week. The children were away at camp. Home was Rochester and she didn't get to New York often so there was a great deal she wanted to do.

Douglas listened to her carefully reticent conversation and when she stopped talking looked at this beautiful, poised, perfectly groomed woman, familiar, yet strange, and interrupted the silence: "You haven't changed much, you know. Only then, you used to wear jeans and tennis shoes and men's shirts, and that shaggy shetland sweater that made you look like an autumn leaf." But he knew he wasn't telling the truth, only trying to conjure up and exorcise a demon.

"I *have* changed," she said.

"So have I."

"You look different."

"You don't. Only," he hesitated, "Only there's something secret in your face that jumps under the skin."

He felt her stiffen and her hand almost jerked up to her face. "You noticed," she said flatly. "The doctors said you couldn't. I got that after my first child, Sean. They said I'd caught a draft or something. Neuralgia, they called it, but I don't think they really knew. They said it would go away, but. . . . "

" . . . but it didn't? Very little does," he said.

She came to his place often, silently coming up the stairs in her sneakers and scratching at the door like a cat that wanted to be let in. Sometimes she slept there on the couch he had bought at the Salvation Army, looking like a stray cat that had wandered into that large white room, to curl up and sleep in front of the great stone fireplace. And as he sat and watched her sleeping, the turning knob of pity became the open door of love, a door slowly opened and a corridor reluctantly entered.

The first time was a snowy cold day so white outside that even his white room paled. He had taken the apartment almost solely because of the fireplace, a big old stonemasoned job of variously shaped and colored stones, carefully mortared into a huge hearth that drew beautifully and burned well. He thought then that he would never be warm again and he wanted fires in the fireplace every day, wood fires, charcoal, newspapers, but flames always leaping up the soot-stained flue. He had a fire going in the fireplace because she liked fires too and he watched her lying on the couch, breathing, her breasts rising and falling beneath her shirt until he touched them and her. After her first indistinct "No," she seemed to stop breathing, her arms stiff at her sides, and it was as if he were alone, a moving aloneness inside that spread like a white wound when he knew there'd been others. For the first and only time he had wanted to be first and only, and the pain of knowing he wasn't was a puritanism beyond his belief or understanding.

She came to him and stayed more often after that, snowy nights when the windows filled with L's of snow, rainy days when the fire roared and they drank red wine mulled with the fireplace poker, and yellow spring mornings when even in the stone city the first raucous birds awoke them. Sometimes he woke early and could not believe that she had happened to him. To surprise his imagination, he would whirl suddenly—as he had often done on patrols—to see if the specter was gone, but she was there, balled into sleep. Sometimes, too, his thankfulness for her rolled him quietly out of bed to dress, to build a fire, and to bring her breakfasts of hot buttered brioches and coffee. The look of astonished gratitude when her eyes opened was an anguish because in them he saw her awakening by others who had treated her in other ways.

And she denied him. At first he thought it might be his fault, the war, his detachment, his wound, even the first sad fitful knowledge that he loved her, but when he tried all he knew—and about that he thought he knew a good deal—there was still nothing: they were never together and it grated like sand in his teeth.

Once, holding her in his arms, he covered her mouth with his, trying to breathe his passion into her like saving someone drowned. "I love you," he'd told her then, aloud for the first time, and she had turned her face into the pillow and wept. When the crying stopped, her face still turned away, him sitting naked on the edge of the bed smoking a bitter cigarette, she'd whimpered into the pillow, not looking at him, not lifting her face, "I can't be with anyone, not anyone, like that. Not even you." He said nothing until, in a muffled whisper that almost escaped him, she ended with, "I can only be by myself."

"Damn it then, be by yourself at least," he'd shouted. He stubbed out his cigarette and lay down next to her. "Go on! Go on! *Any* way. *This* way. With yourself. But *some* way."

Lying next to her, not touching her, he watched: her face buried in the pillow still and turned away, her hands hidden prayerfully beneath, touching herself, her buttocks moving like white waves on a lonely beach, rolling on and on until in a thunder of breathing and a hissing sound of surfeit, she came to rest on that faraway beach, alone and satisfied.

Only then was he sure he'd come back to civilization; only then was he certain he was more than a soldier, a walking wounded; he was a man alive with pain and love. The life-and-death simplicities of Army life were done and the life-and-death complexities of civil life, of that uncivil life that was called *real* life, had once more begun.

And when she told him that before she had only been able to do that alone, never with anyone else even in the room, nor had ever even told anyone, he knew she loved him and hopelessly he cried.

In the elevator Douglas felt himself preening as he saw the same elevator boy glancing at Margaret appraisingly. His body pitched slightly forward on the balls of his feet in a pleasant tension of readiness he used to feel when waiting to return a serve in tennis, and he felt easy and alive, as if he could jump the net in a single fluid motion to accept congratulations for a victory he had earned the hard way.

They took a cab to one of the expensive East Side French restaurants which in the old days he would never have been able to afford, but which, even after all the expense-account years, still left simultaneous feelings of guilt and luxury when he signed the check. They must have looked like lovers, for the headwaiter, who knew him well enough to call him by name—far too well, in fact—gave him an alcove table and then sent the violin and accordion trio over to serenade them as they ate and drank until, discreetly as he could, Douglas gave them a bill to go away.

They avoided talk about the past as if it were a cactus between them and spoke only surface anecdotes about children, homes and business, books and plays, about the food and wine they drank. Douglas felt festive, but kept having to pull his hand back from over his kidney as he felt the jagged scar and probed for that cold spot where once he had known feeling. It's a long time, he reminded himself, as he looked into Margaret's wine-flushed face, eyes slightly glazed and lips moist, and I'm through with that kind of caring—for anything. But outside, walking back to the hotel, when she held his arm and he felt the soft nudge of her breast against his arm, there was a dizzying lurch of happiness in him like the sudden starting of a car, that he knew was more than the wine they had drunk.

As they walked through the city they had known together, Margaret remarked that it was new and different, and she couldn't recognize where she was because they had gone so many blocks down and rebuilt them that her landmarks were gone, her bearings lost. The truth of that, not only for the city, abruptly sobered him. Yet back at the hotel, laughing over a joke he could not remember a moment afterward though the laughter lasted for five minutes, his good humor was restored. They went to his room for a nightcap, and then suddenly, as he poured their brandies, the feeling sluiced away again. He sat across from her on the couch until the long silence embarrassed him into speech. "This," he said, "is what I suppose they call being civilized."

"What do you mean?" Margaret asked, setting her glass down.

"So polite, two acquaintances—or strangers—in a hotel suite after dinner and a pleasant evening. As if we never loved each other, never hated each other, never went to bed together."

"Stop it!" she said sharply.

"Why?"

"Because it's too late, because it's over, and because it's stupid besides."

"It is?"

She nodded and said gently, "It was a long time ago, and it's done."

"I looked for you everywhere . . . " Douglas began. Even in my wife, he thought, until she finally told me I'd have to look elsewhere. In Ellen Hubbard, Isabel Gault, Phyllis Bancroft, though even in his mind this naming of names felt indiscreet, and many more whose names he couldn't even remember. But he hadn't found her anywhere, in any one.

So softly he almost didn't hear, she said, "I looked for you too, for a long time. I tried to get in touch with you at first, if nothing else," she smiled wryly, "to say I was sorry. But no one knew where you'd gone."

"I just left town. I didn't tell anyone where I went," he said.

"Later," she continued, ignoring his comment, "I was too proud to look any more. Besides, by then, I heard you were married."

The quiet in the room was stifling.

"Margaret, Margaret, you gave me back my life. I was a ghost after the war until . . . . "

" . . . but," she interrupted, "you couldn't wait to give me back mine." she stood up and walked to the window, her back turned to him. "When you gave me those Dürer hands, I knew what *they* meant, those strong praying wooden hands. You thought I'd be tied to that forever."

The Dürer hands. Yes, that *had* happened. Walking through the Village one damp fall day, wanting to marry her and unable to reconcile himself to her sudden absences, her bursts of anger, her buried hands and undulating back, he saw those hands in a shop window, one of those three-steps-down-into-the-cellar small stores on Eighth Street. There were other pieces of sculpture, even other Dürer hands—in clay, plaster of paris, terra cotta, lead—but these were hand-honed wood, sensitively and beautifully carved from a wood so light—probably oak or birch—that it resembled real flesh. When he ran his fingers over them, he could almost feel the bones and knuckles, the hard tendons in the back of the hand, the veins beneath the skin. He bought them, cheaply, because the old lady who ran the store thought his khakis made him one of the newly mustered out. The war with Japan had by then been over only a few weeks—the big Bombs had dropped and in that chaos of knowing they tolled the knell of a world, he felt he must move toward some more-ordered future in his own life, to give that chaos some shape and semblance of hope and purpose. But he needed Margaret to do it, and the Dürer hands were his prayer to her, and his gift. With her he was certain he could start again, anew.

When he got to his apartment, he saw the light under the door, heard the fire going, and was glad she was already there. Months before he had given her a key, and sometimes when he came back from stalking the nights, she would be waiting for him. He opened the door now and she was there, hair disheveled, eyes bloodshot, and from the way she wavered up from in front of the fireplace he should have known she'd been drinking, but he was so drunk with his gift he didn't notice.

"I've brought you a present," he said, "a surprise."

"A surprise!" she exclaimed, her voice high and off-key. "Whee, a surprise for Margaret!"

That should have stopped him too. In that year he had learned that when she was drinking she began to talk about herself in the third person. But it didn't. Impatiently, he set the package on a small table and tore off the newspapers the old lady had wrapped the hands in. "Look," he said proudly, when they stood naked in the midst of a pile of newspapers whose headlines seemed ominously black, "aren't those hands beautiful?"

She stood looking down at them, her eyes blinking almost near-sightedly, as if she couldn't quite believe the sight of those two questing poignant hands, and then with a swoop of her cupped hand she knocked them into the fire. "You son of a bitch!" she said softly. "Well, Margaret has her little surprise for you too. I had a one-night stand last night, and I'm glad, I'm glad."

Slowly, he reached over and held her face in his two hands, looking into her tear-blurred eyes. "Why?" he asked slowly, not trusting his mouth to ask more. "Why?"

"Why not?" she answered, her face rebellious and frightened together. He took his hands away from her face and suddenly brought them sharply together again, slapping both her cheeks.

After the door slammed he sat on the couch and watched the Dürer hands in the fire singe, spiral into flame, and then burn into a black and white ash.

In the morning he had gone. He told his landlady he'd send for his things, and he left a small parcel of Margaret's possessions—a couple of books, a pair of torn tennis shoes, a pale green scarf—with her in case Margaret called for them.

At the window, her back still to him, Margaret said fiercely, "I tried, I kept on trying. I made up my mind I wouldn't be like that. Those hands!" He saw the shudder escalate down her back. "Those hands!"

"You never asked what those hands meant to me," he said.

"Could they mean anything else?"

He didn't answer. Whether they had or not didn't really matter.

"You don't know what it was like. I couldn't breathe. I felt like I was being strangled, like I was dying, like— " she stammered "—as if I let myself go I'd lose my name, my brain, myself, and never be able to find any of them again." She turned and faced him. "And I kept looking with each new one, hoping one of them would have the key, because I wanted to give that key to you."

"But you didn't tell me."

"I couldn't."

It was a long silence before she came back to the couch and finished her drink. She smiled at him, not quite reaching the tough gaiety she was searching for. "I didn't stop trying, Douglas, and I had some help. . . . " Her voice trailed off. "What's the point of going over it again? Now. Here. All that's left of that, of me then and of you, is this." She touched her cheek and, as if in answer to her finger, the nerve leaped beneath the skin.

He knew he would ask then, even for "old times' sake," even at the price of destroying it in the asking, and now he knew what the *it* was. He did. She sat hunched over for a long time, as if she hadn't heard him, and then, quietly, she said, "If you want it so much, if you need . . . . " She didn't finish the sentence, she got up instead and went into the bedroom.

He drank his drink slowly, waiting for her to undress, hoping he would have the courage not to go in there, or to go in and say he didn't want it to be that way between them, but he knew he wouldn't, knew he couldn't.

When they were together, her cries tangled with his, her face blindly turned up, the name she cried out was not his. For a while he lay there next to her, shaking with something like inner laughter. Whatever grief had nurtured his love, whatever illusion had fed his sense that Margaret might restore his spirit was a chimera. He no longer could be restored because he no longer cherished anything, not even himself. Not only had she not appeased his hunger, he had deceived himself and her into the belief that the hunger was still there; and it was that absence of yearning, of love, that was most ruinous of all. Once the door had been opened to her, though reluctantly even then; now she no longer had the key; no one did: he didn't have it himself. He had persevered in his detachment, a discipline daily invoked like a prayer until now the full understanding he faced was that his indifference was no longer detachment but truly indifference, no longer a mask but his face. Caroline had been right; nothing beneath his ribs beat that really mattered any longer and for all he knew there was only a vacuum tube under that scar.

He lay there, feeling the ruins of his life around him like the rubble of a bombed city. It was revisiting a cemetery where tombstones marked the last remains not only of the love he had once felt for Margaret, but the love he had felt for life itself. The war, the war, he almost cried out, but which one and with whom? Even as he knew that, he knew it was too late—too late for the wisdom and too late for feeling.

When Margaret got up, he heard her move and watched her dress out of the slits of his eyes, feigning sleep. She touched his cheek with her fingertips, once, gently, and then went out and closed the door quietly behind her, leaving him lying there on the disordered bed in the faint, fading smell of her perfume.

Pluto Is the Furthest Planet

When they first told him, the doctors and then his wife tried to reassure him, but Sanford Tyler was not reassured. Not that he refused to be, but he couldn't for the life of him see that having what Dr. Morrison called cardiac insufficiency was very different from a heart attack. His wife, Viola, tried to explain in her precise, sensible schoolteacher manner that the difference was that he *hadn't* had a heart attack, that he was only forty-three years old, and that once he was rested up, he'd be able to go about his normal life again, but Tyler was by no means convinced. In the meantime, however, it was six weeks of bed rest and then six months of no work, no athletics, and of course—Morrison was half-apologetic, but Tyler thought he detected just a shade of relief in Viola—no sex. Viola moved into one of the twin beds in the guest room, and her clothing, cosmetics, and perfumes went with her. She didn't want to disturb him, she said, and she did have to go on with her job, especially now. It was the cool considerateness and the *especially now* that perturbed Tyler most of all.

No one came to visit because the doctors prescribed complete rest and Viola intended to see that their orders were carried out to the letter. There were some phone calls at first, and a flock of manufactured get-well cards, some of them quite funny, Tyler realized, though his sense of humor also seemed to be suffering comic insufficiency, and the baskets of fruits, candy, and flowers from the office made him feel even closer to the grave than he already did. Tyler did try to take some of the calls, but after a very few he found so little to

say that he let Viola issue the medical bulletins and was relieved
when she gave them on one of the other phones rather than on the
one in his bedroom.

Because he was still a partner, Tyler did have to talk to Charlie
Carson, but all Charlie told him was that things were running fine,
that his work had been divided up among two of the junior partners,
under Charlie's watchful eye, and that he was missed. When Tyler
tried to press for more specific information on cases under consideration, Charlie hedged so that Tyler stopped pressing him to avoid
their mutual embarrassment. Most of the cases he knew were little
more than squabbling for money advantage, and he didn't really
want to know about them, though when Charlie told him that all the
senior partners had agreed to keep him on full salary while he was
out, Tyler was genuinely grateful. But instead of being more easy in
his mind, Tyler was more and more terrified: it was almost as if he
had been left for dead and was watching over a demise that he had
carelessly neglected to consummate. He remembered his own adolescent dreams of frustration and grandeur when he'd vividly imagined his own funeral with everyone dissolved in tears while from on
high he looked down and enjoyed their anguish, their guilt and
remorse. This living experience, however, he found considerably
less soul-satisfying.

The first weeks in bed went by slowly, like the ticking of a clock at
night, so that soon he lost track of time. He lay in bed looking out of
the three squares of window, watching the early autumn skies still
stained with summer pink and green daily deepen into dark winter
reds and slate-gray. Most of the time Tyler slept, or dozed, a half-
waking numbness so restless that it neither gave him a sense of having been gone and come back nor restored him, and left him limp
from nightmares he could not remember. As he drowsed through
the days and the fitful noises of his household's routines, or lay
awake nights listening to the sounds of his heart beating in his ears
and watching the humpbacked black beast outside his window,
pocked with stars, give ground as light scarred its hide and day
whipped it back beyond the horizon, two ideas shaped themselves
out of the welter of half-formed feelings in which he seemed suspended like a bucket in a well, and gradually they took possession of

his mind. The first was a sense of betrayal and the second of isolation; the two were increasingly difficult to separate.

Most of all Tyler felt betrayed by his own body, that bag of guts, bone, and muscle that he now was so separated from and tied to. He'd taken good care of it, fed it well, kept it clean and exercised, and unaccountably it had betrayed him. He had to admit that it had taken a beating during the war and immediately afterward when he was working for the partnership, but no more than many others and a good deal less than most. Worse, he felt betrayed by and isolated from other people. Except for an occasional call from Charlie at the office, in which Tyler thought he heard the note of courteous impatience, there were infrequent calls, no visitors, and virtually no mail. Dr. Morrison saw him twice a week but said no more than "You're doing quite well, Mr. Tyler. You should be up and around very soon," though Tyler suspected that he gave Viola more details, if not much more substance. If he could accept his body's betrayal as an inevitable biological accident, his loneliness was more difficult to deal with.

On the theory that he was sleeping late and not to be disturbed, Viola did not come in to see him in the mornings. From behind his closed bedroom door, he heard her and Mrs. Byrnes get the twins and Eric started to school each morning, and then Viola go off to school herself. After that Mrs. Byrnes brought up his breakfast tray. Eric came home from kindergarten at noon and stayed home for the rest of the day. He'd been warned not to bother Daddy but he came, every day after his lunch, and stood on the landing, not quite silently, casting oblique glances into the bedroom until Tyler called to him. But the boy wouldn't come into the room, or even come near, as if his father had some terrible and contagious disease—mortality, Tyler thought bitterly—that he might pass on to him. "No, Daddy," Eric said, "Mother and Mrs. Byrnes said not to bother you."

"You're not bothering me. I just wanted to see what you look like," Tyler would reply, trying to keep his voice easy and level. The boy stood there for a while, his hands buried in the pockets of his blue jeans, stretching the red suspenders which held them up and kicking one shoe against the other. Then he'd turn and go slowly downstairs. After a while, Tyler heard him singing or laughing or yelling, and could barely refrain from calling him back.

With the twins it was different, perhaps because they were girls, or simply older. In mid-afternoon, as soon as they got home from school, they came dutifully to see him. They were full of their day and talked a streak of people and places he couldn't identify, and though Janice occasionally stopped Jacqueline long enough to inter-ject footnotes, they never quite clarified matters for Tyler. After about fifteen minutes of turning his head from one to the other, as if he were watching them play tennis—the girls always sat on opposite sides of his bed, as if he might otherwise not know which was which—the silence came, then the look which always prefaced their saying, in unison, that they had homework, or chores, or dates, and had to go.

It saddened Tyler to watch them leave, so much like one another, a biological accident he had had to learn to bear, though Viola had always rather enjoyed it, dressing them alike and pleased by the at-tention they always attracted together. They were already, though only just thirteen, so much like women with their lipstick and bouf-fant hairdos. He and Viola had not only quarreled about that but about dates, eye makeup, the length of skirts, and school work, un-til, as if both facts were conclusive, his wife had informed him that his daughters were both "ladies," and that he was becoming an old puritan. Neither accusation seemed decisive to Tyler, but eventually he had given in on the issues that seemed least appalling—the lipstick and the haircuts.

Viola usually came in shortly after they'd left, kissed him lightly on the forehead, puffed his pillows, straightened his blankets, checked the radiator, and kept up a running commentary about her colleagues that made as little sense to him as had the twins' talk. It surprised him that they had so little to talk about except what he might like for dinner, or whether he felt like having his linen changed, that he endured the stream of talk as trying to make him feel, as she had once put it, still "part of the world." After the first few weeks, he had tried to tell her what he felt, fumbling over the words, like a newly blind man gropingly examining things with still clumsy fingers, and she had robustly advised him to read more, watch the television, and not think so much about himself. He'd be all right, it was all simply a matter of time. But beneath her abrupt impatience he sensed her own fear of understanding what he was telling her, or attempting to: she didn't want to know and so he stopped trying to tell her. Though he did try, he couldn't get to reading any of the books he'd bought and saved against the day when he'd have some free time to read, nor could he bear to watch the portable television set which Mrs. Byrnes and Viola brought up for him and which, eventually, at his urging, they took back downstairs for the twins to enjoy.

Because he disliked having things done for him, after three weeks Tyler began to get up to go to the bathroom and was shocked to see himself in the medicine-cabinet mirror. Hollow-eyed, pale, his face seemed a decade older than when he'd last seen it and like the photograph of some remote relative he faintly remembered from his mother's family album years before. It was, he thought, because his hair was uncut, he hadn't shaved and his beard had sprouted a short, dense, grizzled growth that was largely white and made him look Victorian and patriarchal. When Viola finally persuaded the barber to come by one evening to cut his hair, Tyler was grateful, but he refused to have the beard shaved off; the most he would consent to was having it trimmed to look less ragged. The white in it was as shocking a betrayal as his cardiac insufficiency, the death that lurked beneath the skin, the face beneath the mask, and Tyler tried to recall when his stubble had turned white, but all he could remember was a glistening—that could have been water or lather— as he slid the razor over the black hairs every morning.

The shock was great enough so that on the very same day Tyler picked up the telephone and called half a dozen of those he considered his closest friends, but though they all seemed glad to talk to him, none offered to come to visit, and after the first two or three none could be persuaded to drop in to see him. And no one returned his calls. Tyler even called his brother in Arizona long distance, but Clem was too busy with his seed business and his own family to come East for a stay. At first Tyler tried to apologize for them to himself, explaining that there was that primitive superstition lurking in the soul of man that made him fearful of the sick and the dead, the injured and insulted, almost the way his son Eric seemed to be, as if all those could infect the living and healthy with some disease for which there was no cure. And they were all busy with what Viola called "their own lives." But Tyler felt betrayed all the same and more than ever isolated, and the conclusion that no one gave much of a damn forced itself on him like a persistent tackler who had to be fended off with a wary stiff-arm.

One night, lying half-asleep in the dark, the house sounds downstairs so distant they seemed like echoes from another life, Tyler heard the soft shuffling of his son's feet coming up the stairs, followed by his wife's more definite high heels. They paused in front of his bedroom door and Eric called out, "Daddy?"

"Don't wake your father," Viola cautioned in a hoarse whisper, before Tyler answered, "Yes, Eric."

"I want to read you a story."

"Daddy's tired," Viola insisted. "Some other time."

"Daddy reads stories to me when I'm sick," the boy replied stubbornly. "I want to read him a story when *he's* sick."

"I'd like you to read me a story," Tyler called to him.

"All right," Viola agreed, her reluctance an obvious criticism. "You can read Daddy one story. No more and not too long. I'll go downstairs and help Mrs. Byrnes clean up."

Eric sat in the chair next to his bed and Viola turned the overhead wall lamp down so that a cone of yellow light poured down over him. Then she went out. The boy sat quietly, his profile turned, fair skin and cheeks flushed from washing, his dark eyes downcast beneath the broad, pale forehead. Zipped up in red dentons from shod feet to throat, he seemed as whole and healthy and beautiful as a red apple. When he turned his face and eyes and asked, "Which story do you want, Daddy?" something like a separate and beating heart moved inside Tyler. "Any one you like," he answered. Unable to look into his son's shining face, Tyler focused instead on the small, straight fingers that held the book, thinking idly that children's hands and fingers were so elegant and shapely and yet how few adults had hands even remotely beautiful. Blunted by time, he thought, warped by living, and he lay back on the pillow and buried in it his own long, scarred fingers, the two knuckles broken and improperly reset during the war. Staring at the eroded slice of moon outside, he only half listened to his son reading about the solar system, carefully pronouncing each word and occasionally stopping to spell one out so that Tyler could quickly fill it in for him. The book was about the earth and the moon, gravity and sunlight, and the sun and the planets, and Eric read a little about each planet, but he was most fascinated by Pluto. "You know, Daddy," he said, looking up and very serious, "Pluto is the furthest planet from the sun. It hasn't got any light or heat because it's too far away, and it hasn't even got any moons of its own like Jupiter or Saturn." He went on reading about Pluto, as Tyler's mind, snagged on the jagged end of that sentence, caught: "Pluto is the furthest planet. . . ."

"Daddy?"

"Yes," Tyler said, forcing himself to pay attention. "The book says it takes 256 years for Pluto to go around the sun."

Tyler nodded absently.

"Will you be dead then?"

"Yes," Tyler said slowly, "no one lives to 250."

"Not even me?"

"No, Eric, not even you."

"Mrs. Byrnes says that people in the Bible lived until they were 900 years old."

"There were giants in the earth in those days," Tyler declared, and then, seeing his son's puzzled face, went on, "Maybe they measured years differently in those days."

Eric paused. "How do they measure years, Daddy?"

Viola came in then. "All right," she said, "to bed now. Daddy'll explain that another time. Say goodnight."

Eric stood up, closed the book, and set it carefully on the night table. He walked to the bed, leaned his face down, and kissed Tyler. "Goodnight, Daddy," he said, "I hope you get better," as if that was what they'd been talking about. Then, as if he was embarrassed, the boy rubbed his face. "Your beard sticks like pins, like after a haircut. When are you going to shave it off?"

"I don't know," Tyler said. "I like it. Don't you?"

The boy shook his head.

Later, after the lights were out, Tyler heard the boy call to him, and when he answered, Eric said, "You know, Daddy, the book says that from Pluto everything looks little, like stars look to us. Even the sun only looks like a little star from way up there."

"Yes, Eric," Tyler said. "I know." But he didn't ask his son how you could really know what anything looked like to a Plutonian, or to anyone that far out in the solar darkness.

The next morning Tyler got out of bed and, for the first time since he'd been sick, went to the windows. Breathing deeply, he raised his arms and rotated them, feeling none of the nagging weakness that only two weeks before had made even lifting his head from the pillow a task. It was a late autumn day so cold that the sky was white and so clear that in the distance he could see the pond in the park through the leafless trees. The cold had bronzed the last leaves on the privet hedges and turned rhododendron leaves limp and curled, but the grass was still green, though mottled here and there by bare spots and straw-colored patches. Tyler dressed, his clothes feeling new and clean against his skin, so used had he become to pajamas and a robe. He wasn't yet ready to negotiate the stairs, but he walked around upstairs looking out of the windows, watching Eric across the street on his tricycle with two other children chasing the various trucks and cars that drove lazily down the winding street. With his hooded jacket over his head and his white socks flashing between his shoes and his trousers as he furiously peddled his bike, Eric looked like one of Snow White's cheerful dwarfs. As Eric raced back and forth, his open mouth streamed small puffs of smoke in the cold air that Tyler tried to make words of and thought, wryly, that it was like trying to decipher Indian smoke signals in the old Western moving pictures.

Though Tyler's routine remained much the same, the days now seemed to go faster as he watched his son through the windows—digging in the sandbox down the street, swinging from the jungle gym in the back yard, playing hide-and-seek with the neighborhood children. The evenings went more swiftly too, for now that he was out of bed and had begun to come down to the living room,

Eric played long games of dominoes and backgammon with him, cheating outrageously. When Tyler lectured him about it, assuring him that the point was not to win, but to play the game—hearing himself sardonically speak the words that he could neither say with complete conviction nor absolutely reject—and pointing out that Eric could win often and still play fairly, Eric smiled and said, "Yes, Daddy, but I want to win *all* the time"—to which Tyler could give no simple and honest reply.

Viola and the twins badgered the boy for "tiring Daddy out," but Tyler knew that he was drawing strength and vigor from his son, and he thought they knew and were more than a little jealous. As he drew closer to Eric and leaned on him, Tyler was ashamed of it, as if there was something not fair in a grown man taking so much from a small boy, as if their positions were unfairly reversed, but his love for the child rekindled some guttering flame in him, and out of Eric's love for him, and the boy's swift, agile running and jumping, his tough, competitive playing—and cheating—at their nightly games, Tyler knew he drew a new will to live. One evening, when Janice made some casual comment about his "heart failure," he brought her up sharply, correcting it to "cardiac insufficiency," and then Jacqueline started to cry and left the room. Later, before he could fall asleep, Tyler wondered if it had made any real difference, and was it worth having hurt the twins' feelings for. Weren't both terms, to reverse them, simply "failures of heart," or was that a simple, verbal ploy to rob the terror of the simple, physical fact of death?

A week later, the first day after the initial six weeks were ended, Tyler decided to go out. He told no one, not even Viola, but he made his mind up that he would surprise Eric by going in Mrs. Byrnes's place to pick him up at school. When he came downstairs and told Mrs. Byrnes, her silence rang louder than spoken disapproval, and he went through the ritual of telling her that he felt fine and was properly bundled up and really quite ready for a short trip outside. But once he opened the door, he forgot her reproving face altogether in the wave of joy that swept over him with the bite of cold air in his nostrils. "It has taste," he said aloud, "it really does," and Tyler found himself gulping air and walking in what was almost a waltz rhythm.

Everything seemed as if he'd been given new eyes. A scarlet cardinal flushed out of a naked giant hickory tree bolted skyward; a squirrel holding a half-eaten green hickory nut in its paws still seemed to be stalking the bird, and then in disappointed joy dropped it and went from trunk to branch to electric wires, raced across them in staccato dashes like a high-wire specialist, plunged down an electric light pole to the street and was lost in the underbrush. A little way further Tyler found a robin's nest blown down from a maple by the wind. Wisps of it still clung to the branch, and when Tyler knelt to touch the nest on the ground, astonished at how silky it felt, he stroked it gently, then stood up and stepped around it.

Briskly Tyler walked toward the school along the park's edge, stopping on the headland less to rest than to admire the green wintry bay which stretched to the next neck of land where white houses and dark roofs, splotched among the trees, looked almost like a New England village but for the enormous spider of silvered water tower hunched above them. Not a boat was in sight on the choppy waves; only a white cloud of gulls wheeled, banked, and then dived for their prey, skimming the surface like mist. Tyler cut through the park, noting the knotted buds of the young trees, a serene and sealed-off preparation for a coming spring, the arrogant evergreen of jack pine, fir, and hemlock, and the older, leafless trees with ravaged trunks and peeling bark, their heavy limbs creaking like old furniture in the light wind. High over them a lone white gull with black-tipped wings outstretched and unmoving, clearly outlined, sailed, circling.

At the edge of the park the red-brick school loomed up, a modified English fortress with concrete crenelated battlements and cinquefoil decorations, its shadow casting an ornamental fretwork on the ground. A small group of waiting women huddled together in the ragged patch of sunlight next to the exit, and Tyler, unwilling to join them, stood across the street in the shade, though there, for the first time, he felt the chill wind blowing off the park.

Only minutes later the big metal doors swung open and the children came running out. When he saw Eric, Tyler went quickly across the street, but the boy had already turned in the other direction and had his back to him. Tyler walked up behind him, tapped him on the shoulder lightly and said, "Eric, I'm here." The boy turned, arms flailing and fists balled, and Tyler felt him beating his arms and body before he could grab the boy and hold him. "It's me, Eric," he repeated twice, stupidly.

"Why did *you* come? Why didn't you send Mrs. Byrnes?" the boy shouted. "You're sick! You're supposed to be home sick!"

Tyler heard the buzz of women's talk behind him and saw the children turning to stare. "I thought I'd surprise you," he said softly.

"And why don't you shave that silly beard off?" Eric yelled, and then, before Tyler could catch his breath, ran off.

Suddenly chilled and very tired, and wanting to get away from the children's and women's eyes, Tyler followed him at a short distance. Not looking back, Eric now strode along with a dark-haired little girl Tyler recognized as Alison Cartright, one of the neighbors' children. After they walked that way for a while, Eric stopped, and both children waited for him to come up to them. As Tyler approached, he heard his son telling Alison about his "planet book," how if you blasted off in a speedy rocket you'd be all grown up by the time you got to Neptune, and more than thirty years old when you crossed the path of Pluto, the planet that was furthest from the sun.

When Tyler reached them, they stopped talking and Eric took his hand. Together they crossed the street, looking carefully both ways for cars, and walked on toward home.

That evening when Viola returned and Mrs. Byrnes told her he'd gone out, she came to his room and, with his bedroom door shut "so the children won't hear," scolded him in a quiet fury for perhaps twenty minutes until finally, in a voice so cold and final he scarcely recognized it as his own, he stopped her. "I will go out whenever I please, wherever I please. I don't want to hear another word—of advice, caution, or complaint from you, or Mrs. Byrnes, or anyone else. Is that clear?"

"Perfectly," Viola said distinctly. Her mouth, surprised open, repeated in a whisper, "Perfectly." She stood up, automatically smoothing her skirt and brushing her hair from her temples, looking at him with eyes so wide with fear and puzzlement that for an instant he was contrite. Then she left the room.

Tyler lay there for a long time, and when Viola sent the twins to ask him if he wanted any dinner, he said he wasn't hungry. At bedtime Eric came in alone to say goodnight, as if nothing at all had happened at the school. The sight of his fresh, open face made Tyler clutch the boy's shoulders, hold him at arm's length and look straight into his eyes. "Why did you punch me when I came to get you at school, Eric?"

The boy's face closed. He looked down, but he didn't answer, and there was a half-expressed ticlike shrug of his shoulders.

"Did I embarrass you?"

Still no answer.

"Would you like me to pick you up again tomorrow?"

Eric shook his head.

"The day after?"

The boy shook his head again.

Tyler pursued it no further. "Goodnight, Eric," he said, but when Eric moved to kiss him, Tyler almost involuntarily shifted so that his son's lips only grazed his cheek. After the lights were out, Eric called to him in a strange, uncertain voice that Tyler recognized had much in common with the bewildered concern he had read in Viola's face earlier that evening. "Daddy, if you're not sick any more—I mean, if you're feeling better—when are you going back to the office?"

Tyler was silent, thinking that over.

"Daddy?"

"Yes."

"Did you hear me?"

"Yes, Eric."

"What?"

"Yes, I heard you."

"And Daddy?"

"What is it?" Tyler asked, holding down the note of cold irritation in his voice that had crept into his rejoinder to Viola's tirade.

"When you go to the office, shave off that beard, huh?"
When Tyler didn't answer, Eric said, "Please, Daddy?"
"Go to sleep, Eric. We'll see," Tyler replied.

Tyler tossed and turned for a very long time before he fell into fitful dozing, and when he woke with a start, his pajamas pasted to his
chest with sweat, his hair, throat, and face wet, and even his palms
clammy, he remembered the dream he'd been having. Even as he
tried to order it in his mind, it began to recede, just as the gray
ground mist in the dream itself had been swallowed up by the
darkness. For the first time that he could remember, he'd been
dreaming about Italy and the war, and someone chasing him across
a field. Running, he had been driven breathless across a ravine by
machine-pistol fire and into a house which had sprung up out of the
ground. Then an exploding grenade had hurled him through a giant
picture painted on a wall.

Closing his eyes and concentrating all his efforts, Tyler tried not
to let the dream slip away. *What was the picture?* For a moment, he
was sure he was looking right at the Raphael painting of Aeneas carrying old Anchises on his back out of burning Troy, with a woman
staring aghast at the flaming chaos behind, and a small boy accom-
panying them looking up with affectionate anxiety at old Anchises
feebly clinging to his son's power. Then, as Tyler fought to bring the
blurred painting into focus, it faded, and suddenly he remembered
by rote, like a schoolboy, lines he had had to memorize—in Latin
and in English—at prep school, lines he had succeeded in learning
only with great diligence and the surreptitious aid of a trot. *"Facilis
descensus Averni . . ."* he whispered into the dark, silent bedroom,
and then he fumbled, and couldn't remember the Latin until, *"Hic
opus, hic labor est."* But the English came back whole and in a rush:

> The descent to Avernus is easy;
> The gate of Pluto stands open night and day;
> But to retrace one's steps and return to the upper air,
> That is the toil, that the difficulty.

"Sandy?" It was Viola. "Are you all right?" She turned the
night-table lamp on and in the light the last indistinct lines of Aeneas

and Anchises disappeared. She stood there, nervously knotting the blue sash of her dressing gown, and when he didn't answer, she explained, "You were gritting your teeth and groaning like you were in pain. I could hear you in the next room."

"It's all right, Viola, it was only a bad dream. Go back to sleep."

"Do you want me to put the light out?"

He nodded. After she had turned off the lamp, she asked, so softly he could barely hear her, "Do you want me to stay here with you?"

For a moment Tyler wanted to say that it wasn't necessary, but instead, deliberately, "Sure, why not?"

She was soon asleep by his side, warm and breathing regularly, and he was glad she'd offered and that he had not turned her away. Lying back and knowing now he would be unable to sleep until morning, Tyler thought about Eric's Pluto, and Virgil's, and his own, but he knew that one and all were the same—in Troy then, or here and now—and could not be avoided. He'd gone down and even let his son carry him a little way back, but no more. Eric was too young and too weak to do more, and besides it was asking too much of him, and after all he himself was not quite yet an enfeebled Anchises.

Turning on his side, careful so as not to wake Viola, Tyler looked out of the window. Morning was still a long way off, but it would come. When it did he was going to get up, get dressed, and go down to the office. He wasn't going to call Charlie to say he was coming and get no for an answer. And he wasn't going to consult Viola, or Mrs. Byrnes, or the doctors either. Maybe at first it would only be for a few hours a day, maybe even less, but he would make a beginning, and the first thing in the morning, he thought, rubbing his chin and cheek ruefully, as a starter, and as a favor to Eric for services received, he was going to shave.

The Sand Dunes

The dunes rose and fell above the beach, ridged and gullied by the wind, shaping shadows on the bright sands until, matted with coarse green grass, they sheered into the bluffs that overlooked the beach and the flat green ocean. The afternoon sunshine wavered uncertainly on the water and a single gull flew low and clumsily over the slight waves as if looking for something it had lost. From the bluffs Matthew Preston saw it all in one long glance, two or three miles of beach, and it gave him a deep, quiet pleasure.

The narrow trail slipped steeply to the beach and he walked down from the bluff watching Nita's back in front of him with the detached enjoyment the shape of her body gave him, aware only of its propensities for pleasure. On the beach they spread their old army blanket, pegging it down at the corners with lunch basket, thermos, and moccasins. Stretched out in the sunshine, everything seemed tranquil until he remembered that on the bluff behind him the coastguard lighthouse glowered black and white into the quiet blue sky and the radar tower next to it was topped by a cupped-hand gadget ready to receive the news of disaster out of the air.

Lying there, not quite touching her, Matthew thought how often recently Nita seemed to him some wild-eyed straining salmon heaving itself openmouthed upstream to spawn and die. There had been nights when his dreams mixed golden salmon leaping against the current to battle their way to the quiet shallow pools of roe and life with hordes of lemmings plunging like a gray waterfall down to the sea and death. In the weeks since the various tests confirmed that there was nothing physically wrong, the silence between them had grown more pronounced, longer, and their lovemaking an arc of tension whose sparks fizzled out in her tearful anxiety to know if *this was it.* Gil Trudeau's reassurances that there was nothing "functionally wrong," that rest and change of scene might dissipate her nervousness and make conception easier, had not helped. If Nita's disbelief and urgency were emotions he did not quite comprehend—"You're a man," she said bitterly, "how could you understand? How can you know?"—they were also realities he never could quite ignore. And was it simply out of guilt that he imagined too the unspoken accusation of his responsibility for it all, that her barrenness was the result of the abortion she had insisted on in the days when they were living together and that, reluctantly, he had agreed to because she wasn't sure she wanted to marry yet, him or anyone? "My parents are bums, trash," she charged, and she was sure that their same rottenness had been bred in her blood and tissues and would be passed on. Now, feeling the warm sun on his back, the cotton drowsiness around his brain, he realized that those thoughts were always with him in every moment of leisure.

When he awoke she was gone. Stiff with sleep and uneasy because she was away, Matthew went down to the water. It was cold, but once in it he was exhilarated, diving deep to see if he could find starfish on the bottom; but he found none and came up with only the salt water smarting his eyes. When he chugged out onto the beach Nita was on the blanket with a thin, brown-skinned boy in faded blue shorts and gray striped polo shirt. She introduced him as Tommy Bolton and invited the boy to eat with them. Matthew protested that the boy might be expected home to lunch, resenting the additional effort he would have to make for strangers, but the boy said there was no one at home and Matthew, noting the sudden shading of his face, agreed.

While they ate, Matthew watched Tommy Bolton wolf down the tuna fish and egg sandwiches Nita carefully and skillfully set in front of him. Elfin-faced, burned brown by sun and wind, with white-lined crow's-feet around his darting eyes, the boy looked a little old man, wary and uncertain. He loosened up after a while and told them he lived up beyond the lighthouse and coastguard station, and was in the fourth grade because he'd been left back. When Nita asked him why, Tommy said that he hadn't done any homework or studying. Matthew inquired what his parents thought about that and the boy's lips thinned. "They ain't home much," he said, as if that was an answer. He stood up and called over his shoulder to Nita, "I could show you where they's some swell seashells, if you want."

Matthew nodded to cut off her look and watched them walk off over the dunes. Nita was good with children, never condescendingly childish but capable of immersing herself in their world. It was not a talent or interest he shared; most children, even more than most adults, quickly irritated or bored him. Nita came back alone, a paper bag with shells clutched in her hand, saying that Tommy had met another boy down the beach and stayed to play. Obviously she liked the boy, enough so that she was willing to go for seashells with him, and even more to leave him to a new playmate. But she was as always too eager, too intense, too desirous. Nita put the bag of shells down in front of him, its mouth open, and took a conch-shaped one out, intricately carved, beautifully spiny, its hollows a smooth sensuous pink. As he examined the shell, she told him that most of Tommy's friends were grownups, people who came to the beach, where the boy virtually lived. When she'd asked him why, the boy had told her that kids didn't like him much and wouldn't play with him, so what else could he do? Matthew watched the twist of pity and love in her face and turned away to put the conch to his ear and listen to the roaring of the surf which he knew to be the beating of his own blood in his ear but which he could never persuade himself was anything less than deep-sea sounds. Why, Lord, he thought, as he heard the two quick-skip percussions of his blood, can't she relax?

"Did you hear me?" Nita asked.

"Sure," Matthew replied, replacing the shell carefully in the paper bag, "I heard you." What was it in him that so instinctively drew away from that pity and pathos? Its impossibility? Its clear statement that he alone was not enough to her, for her? He wanted children as much as she did; he wanted them more in some ways; and it was not his fault.

Later, stretched out on the blanket, he squinted into the sunlight to watch a gull float above them, remote and unreal, its stiff outstretched wings catching every gust and swirl of air. "So beautiful from far away, so ugly close up," he heard himself say dreamily.

"Who, people?" Nita replied.

"No, sea gulls," he said, pointing.

She turned her dark head up to watch the hovering bird, now motionless above them, and laughed. "Absolutely," she affirmed, "but why so serious and poetic? Didn't breakfast agree with you this morning?" She poured a handful of sand on his chest and ran, and Matthew raced after her, thinking how rarely that sunny spontaneity came to her these days. He tackled her around the knees, letting her fall easily to the sand. They lay there laughing together, panting from the run, their bodies fitting, and he thought that this too was part of it, part of the golden, twisting salmon and that you couldn't have this without the other. Then Nita's face, as if in response to his thought, went somber, and he followed her look to the top of the bluff where Tommy Bolton and a taller blond boy were running. Their shouting floated down to the beach, hollow-sounding and distant. "Bang! Bang!" They shot each other cowboy fashion, index fingers rigid and thumbs hooked. "I got ya. You're dead."

The blond boy fired from the hip, Tommy spun, held his stomach as if it ached, then jackknifed over and rolled down the bluff head over heels. Matthew ran for the bottom, Nita right behind him, but when they got there the boy was standing, brushing the sand off. Then he whirled, brought a make-believe rifle to his shoulder, and shot at the blond boy on the bluff. "Got ya! Yah!" The blond boy came rolling down the bluff a little distance away. As he stood up, the cry "Lawrence! Lawrence!" echoed behind them and an agitated couple, obviously the boy's parents, rushed up. The woman began to brush the boy's hair and shoulders, hitched up his shorts, shouting all the time, "You could kill yourself like that. . . ." She paused for breath, her face contorted, then turned furiously on Tommy Bolton. "It's all your fault, you little . . . you . . . beachcomber! I ought to. . . ." she raised her hand to slap him, but her husband stopped her. "You better go away, Sonny. I don't want you playing with our boy, understand?'

Tommy nodded mutely.

The man turned to them. "Letting children take such chances. You people ought to be ashamed." Before they could reply the indignant parents were stalking down the beach, the boy between them, both reprimanding him at once. When the boy turned to wave good-bye to Tommy, his mother shook him roughly around and his father brandished his fist in the air. "Don't forget," his trembling voice rang, "you stay away from Lawrence!"

Tommy Bolton was crying and Nita tried to comfort him, explaining that they hadn't really meant what they said, that they were only afraid that their son might be hurt, but Tommy sobbed that he did it almost every day and never got hurt. "But you might," Nita cautioned. "It's a long fall."

"It's only sand," Tommy insisted, pulling away, and before they could stop him, he ran up the side of the bluff, his small frame bent against the steep incline. When he got to the top, Matthew called up to him to go on home, but the boy jumped, tumbling down a helter-skelter of brown arms and legs, rolling to a stop almost at their feet. Then Tommy got up, standing stiff-legged away from them, saying, "I told yuh it was all right," before running away down the beach.

Nita stood trembling and pale, her skin goose-bumped until he rubbed her arms to warm and comfort her, and she whispered between white lips, "You can't even take care of them if you do have them, you just can't do it right."

"Kids manage," he said.

"No. You can't watch them every minute."

"But that's not the point, Nita."

"What is the point, Matt?" she asked, her jade eyes flat.

"To teach them to take care of themselves."

"Like my parents taught me?"

He shook his head. "No, teach them to take care of themselves."

"You mean not to be afraid?"

"No, not to be unreasonably afraid."

"Is that what your parents taught you?" The cutting edge to the words was more challenge than question, and he thought about it for a while before answering, helping Nita into her beach coat and putting his arms around her. For an instant he thought about his parents, as he so rarely permitted himself to do now, saw their faces as if they were alive, and then set the whole picture away from him as if he were returning a faded family portrait to the bottom drawer of a dresser.

"They taught me to be afraid only of feelings," he said, meaning to make a joke of that, but realizing that it was altogether true, "not of things, or of physical danger. My father liked to see me play dangerous games—lacrosse, ice hockey, football—but he didn't like me to get *messed up with people*—as he put it." That same love of danger had made his father successful in business; the same thing Tommy Bolton did in miniature, rolling down a cliff, his father had often done in business. "Risk," his father had lectured him, "*risk* capital. They forget the first and remember only the second. It takes guts and judgment to take risks, and it pays off."

"And your mother especially didn't want you to get messed up with girls, I suppose," Nita added. Her voice was full of venom, though she'd never known either of his parents. It was the way she always spoke about them, as if their very existence was an affront to her; it was the way she always talked about his going into the business instead of practicing law, for which she blamed them. It was as if their concern for him was something she could neither accept nor forgive; because she'd been cheated of such concern herself, she assumed their feelings must have been a tyranny. But she was wrong. His mother had wanted him to marry, to have children, though, looking at Nita now, Matthew wondered if his parents would have approved of her. Probably not. His father would have balanced his palm like a scale to indicate that Nita was too unreliable for him. But what difference did it make anyway? He was his parents' son, surely; but he was his own man and responsible. And Nita was responsible too, whatever her parents had been and done.

That night at the restaurant where they ate regularly, Nita asked their waitress about Tommy Bolton. Flora was a local girl and knew all about them Boltons, the no-goods, and the boy'd turn out just like em. Jim Bolton was a carpenter, married to Evalyn Groves—she used to work up to Boston in an office—and the boy was born but seven months after. People round there weren't so dumb they couldn't count. "Anyway they's never home with the boy, let him tramp around all summer on the beach, then ship im up to his Grammer's in town for winters. Always in bars drinkin like fish, no wonder the boy's turnin out bad. Bright lad too. Neighbors don't let their kids play with im and I don't blame em none either. Why the boy told the Harper girl bout how his folks . . . not that it's the boy's fault, I s'ppose. . . ." and she went off in mid-sentence for their dessert.

"Tommy's a real local scandal," Nita said lightly, but the brittle sentence shattered on the table between them. Matthew saw how upset she was when she sent Flora for a pack of cigarettes and began to smoke one from the end of another, unspeaking, unapproachable. She never talked about it, never said it straight out, not that mere framing of the sentences would solve things; but at least if once she could clear the air by talking about what kind of people her parents were, say how much she hated and resented them, she might be able to ask what that had to do with her now and get some answers.

Later, for the first time on the vacation, they went to a bar in town and sat quietly in a booth over two sweating cold beer mugs, not talking, though twice she put the tips of her fingers against the tips of his as if hoping some connection might be made, some current leap between them. And though he took her chill hands in his and rubbed them to warm them, kissed her palms, they remained cold.

A voice boomed across the dimly lit bar. "Matt! Matt Preston!" A man bulked over them whom Matt couldn't recall having seen before. "Don't you remember me?" The fat face creased into a thousand smiling wrinkles. "George. . . ."

" . . . Warner!" the name started to his lips, dredged from some forgotten corner of his mind, and the face he'd known at Yale seemed to start lean and young from beneath the middle-aged features before him. "George Warner," Matthew repeated, marveling that he remembered at all and noting that Warner took that to be delight in seeing him again.

The Warners, it turned out, were staying at a place a mile or so up the road from their cabin. After introductions, they sat and talked and drank. Kay, George's wife, was a tall, svelte brunette who, though she wore tailored slacks and a white blouse, managed to look as if she were in evening dress, and she provided a wry ironic running commentary to George's boastful description of their life. He reminisced about Yale and told how he'd met Kay in New York, about their Sutton Place apartment, about how he was now vice-president in a public relations agency and doing very well, very well indeed. Kay cut him off to describe her interior decorating business, which apparently was doing even better. Between swallows of beer, George said patronizingly, "Yep, my bride . . ." Matt saw Kay wince " . . . has turned into a great little competitor of mine. Runs her own business, big business too."

"George can't bear the fact that I make more money than he does," Kay asserted flatly.

Matthew turned away from their open hostility to stare into his beer mug and heard Nita, as if to make up for not having spoken more than half a dozen sentences up to that point, inviting the Warners to a beach supper the next day. They accepted and went on as before, undiverted.

"Kay's a great little kidder," George commented. "You mustn't mind her sense of humor."

"And George is a funny man too," his wife retorted. "Ask him and he'll tell you."

George reached around Kay's shoulders and squeezed her to him, his knuckles showing white, and suddenly, strangely, they both began to laugh, a laughter loud, yet private, that excluded and embarrassed him.

Walking through the dark back to their cabin, Matthew said, "I'm sorry you invited them."

"So am I," Nita confessed, "but I couldn't stand their going on like that. Was he that way at school too?"

Matt remembered George Warner working at being a big man on

campus, wearing his white sweater with the varsity Y on it, and never forgiving him quite because he was seeded first on the tennis team and George second. That must still rankle because he'd mentioned it at the bar, twice. Warner'd been considered a great ladies' man in those days too, usually squiring the most striking girls where he could be seen with them. Matthew shrugged. How could he answer a question like that? And what did a few fragmentary recollections of a man at college remembered through adolescent eyes mean anyhow?

He awoke suddenly in the middle of the night, missing Nita next to him, and saw her standing at the window looking out to the sea. He heard the crashing of the waves on the beach, heavy and rhythmic, and not to startle her, called softly, but she seemed not to hear. He got out of bed and walked behind her, putting his arms around her and nuzzling her neck; and she shuddered.

"I hate them," she said hoarsely, "I hate them. They're just like my. . . ." She shouldered him away and then turned, holding her breasts with her hands as if they were too heavy and painful to bear. "And I'm just like them. I'd give it to the next generation, just the way they will, like a plague. I'd only make . . . another Tommy Bolton." Her teeth bared, her hands cupped over her breasts, she seemed like some fierce, berserk animal guarding and displaying her wounds, proud and crazed together.

The morning was unbelievably still and peaceful. Nita went walking with Tommy Bolton in search of more seashells. They brought back two dried starfish, sand-colored and stiff, with a spiny loveliness that made Matthew want to caress them. When they left the beach for lunch, Tommy promised to borrow rods and reels so that they could fish in the afternoon. Matthew said he didn't fish and Tommy, delighted, promised to teach him to surf cast for striped bass.

When they came back to the beach in the afternoon with a basket full of food for the evening meal with the Warners, Tommy was waiting with the rods and reels. While Nita nervously wrapped the thermos of iced martinis in a towel and hid it from the sun—drinks, strong drinks, she insisted, were an absolute necessity if she was to bear the Warners politely—Matthew went down to the water with Tommy. Carefully the boy showed him how to bait and cast, trying hard to teach him the flick of the wrist that the boy himself did automatically when casting. They stood in the water a hundred yards or so apart and fished in a serenity of sun and surf, staring at the thin seam where sea and sky were stitched together. Matthew felt close to the boy and by the relaxed way Tommy Bolton held himself, the look of quiet pleasure on his face when he caught two striped bass and a small skate and showed them for approval, Matthew knew that the boy was also feeling close to him. He forgot about the Warners, he forgot about Nita, the nighttime Nita, he forgot the grim lighthouse and the cupped waiting hand of the radar antenna on the bluff; but he couldn't forget Nita hidden behind her dark glasses, knitting and watching, and smoking cigarette after cigarette on the beach behind them.

When Tommy said he had to return the borrowed rods and reels, Matthew watched him disappear up the bluffs with a pang of loss. He went back to the blanket to watch Nita concentrate on the argyle slipover she was knitting for him, put off by her painstaking, lip-biting preoccupation with the multicolored wools and the clicking needles. And then the Warners arrived. Kay took off a blue terry-cloth robe to reveal a beautiful suntanned body in a black bikini. Nita's stare at Kay's figure and the simultaneous disapproval of the two slender bands of black material, one held by a single black bow at the back, the other by two identical bows on the hips, touched him. And there was disdain on Kay's face as she looked down on Nita's knitting.

George smirked and said, "She's something, eh, Matt?"

"Sorry we're late," Kay apologized, ignoring him. "George was playing tennis. . . ."

" . . . doubles, not much for singles any more," George interrupted ruefully, "getting too old. . . ."

" . . . and too fat," Kay added.

Matthew saw the finger-shaped bruises on her arm, dark beneath the skin, like a birthmark or bloodpromise, and above, in the hollow of her shoulder, the same purpling bruises that were the clear outline of a mouth. He remembered the squeezing white knuckles in the bar the night before and that unaccountable laughter; and he looked away, but as his eyes slid past Kay's something in them acknowledged his notice and was unashamed.

"Bang, bang," came Tommy's shout as he ran up from behind, firing from the hip, and Matthew was grateful for his interruption.

"Your son?" Kay inquired, turning to Nita with a gesture that said more clearly than words that it would be *your* son who does that kind of thing.

"No," Nita replied solemnly, "we don't have any children. This is a friend of ours, Tommy Bolton." Though she had introduced the boy, their talk excluded him, and Tommy, sitting and listening, soon grew restless. He wandered down the beach to skid stones over the incoming tide. Matthew wished he could join rather than listen to George Warner's business exploits or watch Kay's perverse joy.

"The Bolton boy has bad manners," Kay commented sharply, as if that was what they'd been talking about. "He looks like one of those kids in those dreary Italian movies. Where did you find him?"

"Leave it to Kay to say things like that," George remarked. "Hates kids. Positively can't stand them. Only interested in men, not little boys." There was a note of sorrow and incomprehension in his voice and his features went slack.

"That's George's way of saying I don't want children—and he does," Kay countered. "George wants a son—to teach tennis to, I suppose."

"Might ruin her figure," George said shortly. The pain and puzzlement in his face made it, for the first time, something human and enlisted Matthew's momentary sympathy. "I guess it might, at that," George added.

Nita rushed in too quickly to explain about Tommy, and George was taken with Tommy's having watched his parents—as George summarized it—"in the act." Matthew was appalled that Nita had blurted that kind of gossip and tried to forestall her in mid-sentence; but she was clearly so upset with the Warners' quarrel about having children that she forged ahead without listening to him, and probably, he thought, without listening to herself. By the time Tommy came back, shuffling his feet through the sand, George had had three martinis and was half through a fourth. He was proclaiming loudly that he had endured all kinds of torments from the boys in his office when Kay had gone by herself to Paris to buy some antiques at auction. "Hallo, Tommy old boy," he called, interrupting himself, "come have a drink."

The boy squatted at the edge of the blanket, his legs darker than the khaki. "You got a girl, Tommy?" George asked.

Tommy said nothing.

"Bet you got lots of girls, haven't you?" George insisted.

The boy stared at him, unblinking eyes like beach pebbles.

"And you take them up to the shacks, or on the beach . . ."

". . . George!" Kay's voice warned.

". . . and you touch them here," he patted his wife's knee, "and then here," he stroked her hip, "and then . . ." he cupped his hand slowly over her breast, his eyes never leaving Tommy's face. Tommy moved so quickly his hand was a brown flutter and the bikini fell away from Kay's body, leaving a corner of darkness like a staring eye in the soft white flesh of her belly. "You mean like that, Mister?" the boy asked in a tight little voice. Slowly, with boyish dignity, he walked away down the beach. There was a silence until Kay, in a slow dead voice said, "He . . . he . . . touched me."

George stood up from the blanket, swaying slightly, as if in a wind, and finished his martini. "I guess I have to teach that youngster a lesson."

Matthew got up too, knowing he was going to enjoy knocking George Warner down if he so much as moved in Tommy Bolton's direction, but Kay, her voice metallic now, said, "Sit down!" George stood openmouthed and she repeated, louder and sharper this time, so there would be no mistaking that it was a command: "I said, sit down!" And George sat.

After a time Nita said something about Tommy's being only nine years old, placatingly, almost piteously, as if she were asking something for herself, but no one said anything in answer. They sat on the blankets and watched the sun dive toward the horizon, the water growing grayer and colder, the backs of the dunes throwing long shadows into the sand hollows and the long faces of the bluffs overcast by oncoming dusk.

A pebble skipped a burst of sand near them, then another, and another still. Tommy was throwing them from the shadows of a nearby dune. In a few moments the boy dashed toward them from another direction and tossed a dead skate just a few yards from their blanket. As George again began to get up, Kay barked, "Just ignore him. He wants attention, that's all. Ignore him and he'll go away." George sank back on the blanket.

"He's probably sorry," Matthew brought himself to say, "and that's his way of saying he wants to be forgiven." He knew how the boy was feeling; after all he *was* only nine, a child. But it was more than that. It was as if he and Nita were so intimately involved that they needed Kay's forgiveness for themselves as well as for the boy. Forgiveness? For what? he asked himself furiously. For even knowing the boy? Or for permitting a child to share, even for a moment, their squalor and corruption, their beautiful world of adults?

"Forgiven?" Kay pronounced the word as if its meaning had either passed her by or escaped her altogether. Matthew knew she was talking not about Tommy but about George, and for the first time he really understood the bruises and the deliberately degrading hand on her breast: that had *not* been for Tommy's benefit alone.

"Look at that nutty kid now," George muttered. Matthew looked and saw Tommy at the top of the bluff, skirting the edge, teetering, pretending to lose his balance and regaining it, swaying with outstretched arms on the edge like a tightrope walker.

"I told you he just wanted attention," Kay said spitefully.

"Well, then," Matthew said, "why not give him some?" and out of the corner of his eye he saw Nita's instinctive recoil. What was wrong with giving someone attention if he needed it that badly, especially a child? Was it really all that humanly expensive?

"He's falling," George yelled.

Matthew turned again and saw Tommy rolling, almost lazily, down the bluff, his brown arms and legs out of control going like the spokes of a wheel without a rim. He raced for the bluffs and then he heard the boy's scream. By the time he got to him, the boy was wrung strangely out of shape, one leg folded under his back. George camp up, puffing, suddenly sobered, and saying, "Broken, isn't it?" But there was something short of pity in his face.

"Go up to the coastguard station," Matthew said, hearing the same cold tone of command in his voice he'd hated in Kay's, "and get a stretcher." Clumsily, George ran up the bluff and then Nita and Kay arrived. Kay shuffled uncomfortably while Nita, eyes narrowed, stood by smoking. Then, abruptly, Tommy Bolton leaped to his feet and ran away from them, turning back only to taunt them with an obscene gesture of his fist and a high-pitched fluting, "I fooled ya, I fooled ya."

Two coastguardsmen brought the stretcher down moments later but Tommy, out of their reach, stood grinning silently, ready to run, a few hundred feet away from them. Matthew tried to explain but the two young coastguardsmen didn't like it and they quit grumbling only after George offered them martinis. Soon they had folded up the stretcher and were trudging back up the bluff. Matthew, silent, could not take his eyes off the boy. He felt betrayed, rebuffed, and then he saw Tommy's face change as if he was about to shout something, but the boy seemed to change his mind and his mouth shut, tight. To avoid looking at his face Matthew turned and saw George pouring himself another martini while Kay watched him, her face unguarded for a moment and filled with contempt. George looked up and caught her expression. He stopped, stunned, and then awkwardly but deliberately his arm swung up and emptied the martini into his wife's face.

Behind him Matthew heard Tommy's laughter rise high and broken and he knew the boy had seen and understood; but then, next to him, Nita began to shout hysterically, "You horrible boy! You monster! Get out of here!" and she ran crazily toward Tommy Bolton. It was twenty yards before Matthew caught her, and even as he brought her down to the sand he saw Tommy standing there, like a stricken bird, his hands like a prizefighter's raised in front of his face, waiting, waiting.

They lay there in the sand for a long time, their bodies heaving with their exertions, until Nita sat up and went back for a cigarette. With it in her mouth, she leaned hovering over him for a light. Matthew struck a match for her and past its flame he looked straight into her eyes, two pitiless and pitiful fragments of jade.

Polonaise

That weekend I'd reserved to myself. My wife had been feeling tired
and rundown and I'd arranged for her to take my sons to her sister's
farm in Connecticut for a long weekend. The Torczyn invitation
came in the mail days after the arrangements were completed, a typi-
cal Torczyn printed card that looked much like an invitation to a
children's birthday party, and I saw Sally's relief plain on her face.
It got her off the hook in two separate ways. Because she was always
more than a little shamefaced when she left me to my own devices,
even if it was only for a single night out at a professional meeting or
for a shopping jaunt, especially guilty when the housekeeper was to
be off at the same time, Sally urged me to go to the Torczyn party.

"After all," she reminded me, "you'll be home alone for three
whole days! Even Marthe will be off. What will you do with yourself?" In spite of my protestations that I liked being alone, or perhaps because of them, Sally behaved as if I could not get myself a
meal or make a bed, and would perish of loneliness and boredom. If
there was something genuine in her concern and something surreptitious in her sense of dereliction, real or fancied, there was also her
sense of foreboding; as if after twenty-five years of marriage I
should find that I could, in solitude, dispense with her person and
presence, as if I might, somehow, somewhere—in her absence and
as a result of it, discover that *femme fatale* whose passionate concern would once and for all put me beyond her reach.

If Sally was guilty and uncertain about leaving, she was also relieved, because she didn't like the Torczyn kind of party; too much drinking, too much food, too much noise, too much of the kind of emotional effusion and confusion which Sally found unappetizing and inelegant. Just as the fascinations of molecular biology, her field, and its mathematical abstractions were far more elegant than the grosser realities and disorders of the human body, so she preferred social encounters which did not call upon the deeper resources of her feeling or strain her self-control. It was a useful preference for the professional biologist, a preference she shared with Marek Torczyn, one of the less obvious reasons why both were so good at their jobs, why both had done such good research for the laboratories of the pharmaceutical corporation which paid their salaries. But such a trait, with all its elegant intellectuality, lacked the hearthlike quality for other human beings whose extremities might be cold and who might wish to warm at human fires.

When I came home from work on Friday evening, Sally and the boys were already gone and the house did, indeed, seem empty and echoing; but I soon had the Mozart playing and enjoyed the cold chicken and salad Sally had prepared and left me for dinner, that reminder of her role that she could not altogether forego, and the bottle of cold Soave I had shored up against the evening.

For the weekend I had jotted down a list of long-delayed household chores. The garden was its usual October shambles, crying out for raking, cleaning, pruning, fertilizing, liming, and all the rest of the necessary and time-consuming tasks which preparation for winter entails. We had had a gardener until a few years before when a couple of extra inches around the waist and Sally, impressed by what some of her knowing medical colleagues had written about physical exercise as a means of preventing heart attacks in the middle-aged, prevailed on me to do the gardening myself. Writers are, and have to be, sedentary creatures—they spend a large part of their lives sitting on their tails at a desk—so Sally always was urging me to play tennis or squash or go for a swim, none of which I did. So she had let the gardener go; she knew I wouldn't let things die, or wouldn't if I could help it.

By late Saturday afternoon I was able to check off most of the items on my list: the garden was, if only for a solitary hour, clear of red and yellow beech, maple, and locust leaves; the roses were pruned and mulched, the grass and shrubs fed against the long winter ahead, the entire bucolic autumnal ritual indulged in and endured. Storm doors and windows had been hoisted to replace the screens and all the rest of the battening down for the cold had been completed. I sat in the living room, the curtains drawn against the wild orange anger of a setting sun, and permitted myself the cool luxury of a Mozart piano concerto and a quiet bourbon. No sooner had I leaned back into my favorite wing chair, with a half-groan, half-sigh of contentment, full of the spurious sense of achievement that completing such minor myriad tasks gives, than the telephone rang.

"Professor Wallace?"

I didn't recognize the voice and the *professor* put me off. It had been more than a dozen years since I had left teaching and I couldn't imagine what ghost had come to pay a call. "This is he," I replied hesitantly, the whisky abruptly cold in my stomach.

"Martin? I fooled you, hah?"

It was Leszek Stawinski, an old friend, a poet and translator of note, and, if one must make such catalogues, my favorite Pole. "You fooled me all right, Leszek," I confessed, "but you know that's not very hard to do."

"But you answer to professor!" Mock outrage.

"Well, I was one, a professor that is."

"Yes, so you were, Martin," Leszek said, as if he'd forgotten, though I knew he hadn't. For Leszek, in spite of his own anti-academic tirades and rebellious anti-establishment posture, retained that European respect for the titles and honors of the academy. "You are coming to the Torczyn party? We'll stop off and you can drive us there. Anne and I will be at your place in one hour exactly. Okay?"

I remembered Leszek blind drunk at the last Torczyn party, what he had done then, and how much more anxious Anne would be this time. And how Leszek hated to drive, always got lost in the wilds of Long Island's suburbs once he got off the clearly marked parkways

that brought him down from Nyack. They were two of the very few
old friends I had left, so I felt called upon to say for them to come
ahead: I knew I couldn't get away with not going to the Torczyn
party.

Before he rang off Leszek told me that I'd particularly enjoy this
party because Marek and Maria were giving it for the Polish novelist
Stanislaw Danzig, who was now visiting the States on one of the
government cultural-exchange programs. Among the half-dozen
best-known and most talented Polish writers, Danzig was an old
Warsaw friend of the Torczyns and an intimate of Maria's sister Ursula for more than twenty years.

I had not seen the Stawinskis since early summer. Their faces had
changed in those months but the greetings and embraces were warm
as always. Only after I had taken their coats, given them chairs, and
unthinkingly offered drinks, which Anne refused for both of them,
did I see the new small red scar on Leszek's left cheek, over the bone
which supported the horn rim of his glasses. The scar made his boyish
ascetic face more wounded and wrathful-looking than ever; it added
to the rage of feeling and perception I knew pulsed behind his green
eyes and that was fused with a flinty warmth that often became, unaccountably, sentimentality. My Slav soul, Leszek was wont to explain, half-boastfully, half-apologetically, flaying the Anglo-Saxon
"coldness" he had never liked or understood; and in part paying a
debt to his first wife, who was a bona fide Anglo-Saxon. In spirit the
man who had survived the Polish debacle of 1939 and the Soviet
prison camps of Central Asia, the man who had endured a first marriage until his son was grown, and then endured the divorce which
separated him from that only child he loved more than anyone in the
world—except Anne—coexisted uneasily with the youth who still
sang "Stenka Razin" or "Moscow Nights" in Russian in a tenor
voice filled with tears, a voice that sometimes, especially when he was
drinking, broke with the weight of his emotions. When deepest in his
cups, he sometimes sang—in English—"Mein Yiddische Mama" in
the heartrending voice that only a boy orphaned from the age of eight
who had spent most of his youth in a variety of rigid, harsh Polish
Catholic orphanages could manage. But why "Mein Yiddische
Mama," I could never fathom. And who was to say which of his

qualities, the "soft" or "flinty," had most helped him to survive the rigors of his life? Not I. Surely not I.

Leszek touched his fingertips to the new scar and told me that a surgeon had excised a cyst during the summer. He asked, for Leszek was vain about his lean good looks, if the scar was so noticeable. Obviously I had been staring. I adopted the rough style of our humor and told him it made the rebellious cast of his face more like that of the monstrous St. Just, that rebel he professed to admire extravagantly. "That scar's no revolutionary change," I remarked.

"Funny," he said, refusing to laugh.

Anne seemed more changed, although there were no visible scars. She wore a red velvet dress I remembered from at least ten years before, the tight bodice molding the fine shape of her shoulders and breasts, the skirt flaring away from her slender girl's waist; I could see where the skirt had been shortened to meet the fashions, showing more of her short yet exquisite legs. Her puritanical head was older and seemed out of place on that still young, still sensual body: her fine black hair swept back into a matronly pompadour proudly revealed the gray streaks; beneath, the small peregrine falcon's sharp nose and hooded eyes were weakened and softened by the disappointed mouth and uncertain chin. Her skin, lined and carelessly powdered, had the same pallor as the antique cameo that hung on a long chain between her breasts, face turned in, blank silver back out. More than anything Anne looked like the old Russian gentry of the postwar Tsarist emigration during its shabbier days in Berlin and Paris.

I wanted to lift the downturned ends of her mouth into a smile, but, already wreathed in cigarette smoke, she seemed a remote sibyl, tiny, regal, and lost looking. Despairing of my own resources, no novelty for me in life in general and in human relations in particular, I excused myself and went upstairs to get the gift I had brought back from Japan for her. She took the damascene pin from the unfinished wooden box, held it in her cupped palm, as if the classical bamboo pattern spoke something only to her, and murmured, "Beautiful." The smoke brought tears to her eyes but no smile graced her lips and she didn't try the pin on. Leszek, glancing awkwardly at me, said, "You see, Anne, I told you Martin wouldn't forget you." Just what slight of the soul that unction was supposed to heal I didn't know, but the damascene pin did not seem quite the kind of remembrance Anne required.

On the way to the Torczyns, Leszek talked of how much he wanted to get the hell away from the cities. Nyack was too close, there wasn't enough space, the air and river were polluted, there were too many people, and it was too expensive. Over the summer, while I had been traveling in Japan, they had driven through New England, Leszek for the first time, and there he had discovered the setting in which he wished to live, a landscape with the bleak rockiness and dour pines which, he said, reminded him of his area of Poland. In great detail Leszek explained how, up in Maine, taxes, food, land, and houses cost half of what they did in New York; and how, once they settled in there, he'd be able to give up translation, which he hated and did for a living, or at least give up a large part of it, so that he could devote himself to his own poetry.

"You knew how Leszek is, Martin," Anne said shrugging. "Now that we've got this house fixed up and comfortable, he wants to move. When we get the one in Maine in shape, he'll want to move farther north, to Nova Scotia."

"It's exile's foot," I said. "Worse than athlete's foot. Always itching."

They ignored me. "Now, honey," Leszek began, "you know that's not," but I cut off the long protest by announcing that we had arrived. I parked the car in bloody pools of leaves and we got out and walked up the drive. The Torczyns were always building new additions to their house, or taking pieces off, or rerouting the driveway, or reshaping the garden, so that I didn't even recognize the house. Leszek rang the bell and a woman I didn't know came to the door.

"Hello," I said, "you don't recognize us." It was clear that she didn't and was puzzled by our breezy manner.

"Come in," she said, hesitantly, "come in please." Leszek spoke to her in Polish but she seemed uncertain still.

"Aren't the Torczyns expecting us?" I inquired.

"Ahha! The Torczyns," the woman exclaimed, her face relieved and smiling now. "Wrong house here. Torcyzns live next door."

We apologized, Leszek taking the formal lead and, having kissed her hand gallantly, he led us out. Cutting across the lawn to the Torczyns' we laughed like children. "Did you see that?" Leszek whispered hoarsely, unable to control his guffaws. "She didn't even know who we were, but she greeted us like old friends and invited us in."

"Polish hospitality," Anne commented wryly.

"I didn't know Marek and Maria had any Polish neighbors," I said.

"That's because Maria's always complaining that she has no one to talk to, that she's sick of the little minds and conventions of suburbia, that Americans have acquaintances but no friends," Anne mocked Maria's histrionic manner.

"Something like that. Maria always manages to accuse us of not being good 'European' friends, though it's always *we* who call *them*, or we who drop by to see them. If we don't, months pass without our hearing from or seeing them," I laughed. "It makes Sally furious."

"It should," Anne remarked.

"*You* should be more sympathetic to Maria," Leszek advised. "She and Marek moved into this neighborhood so they could have some Poles around, and a Polish parish church. They wanted to see that the children wouldn't lose the language or the traditions altogether."

"Maria feels only her own loneliness," Anne retorted. A bitterness edged her voice that I had heard before and been moved by, as I was now, again.

This time it was the right house and Marek Torczyn greeted us with that formal manner and British-accented English which, with his own curious diffidence and disdain, was enough to make me feel slightly uncomfortable about being welcome. Always. Marek perennially seemed to be talking to people from some great height where he stood alone, and I was hard put to it to discover if that was because he spoke from some special sense of detachment twice removed or simply the illusion created by his height. One of the handsomest men I had ever seen, Marek was over six feet three inches tall, powerfully but gracefully built, with the lean aristocratic good looks which distinguish Polish rulers from their peasantry, and make them seem almost an altogether different race, which in fact they might well be. The differences were great but perhaps nowhere clearer than in Marek's nose—lean, aquiline, with slim slashes of nostril—and Leszek's ski-jump thicker nose, softer, with rounded nares: they might have represented the two Polands, the two cultures, town and country, gentry and serf, which had struggled on that bleak plain for a thousand years and which were perhaps symbolized unwittingly by the two-headed Polish eagle—but the resemblances were only physical.

"We've just met your neighbors," I told Marek.

"Have you?"

"I led Leszek and Anne up the garden path to the wrong house," I added. "Didn't recognize yours. You've changed something again, haven't you?"

"No," Marek answered. "You just haven't been here for such a long time, you don't remember."

"Oh come on, Marek, don't talk like your wife," I said acerbically.

He laughed. "See what intimacy will do." Then, ruefully, added, "Well, proximity anyway."

Marek ushered us into the living room where Maria, in the rich linguistic mélange of an English full of accents and intonations which combined deep-throated Polish consonants and upper-palate French vowels, exclaimed, "Ahha, they are here!" She embraced Leszek even before he could manage to kiss her hand and I saw the tremor of lip beginning that Anne swiftly suppressed. "Leszek," Maria cried, "how I am missing you! I am happy you come already. And you are missing vodka. Four, five rounds already." She squeezed him quickly. "Is very good to see you." She only just touched Anne's shoulders and grazed her cheek. "Anne—" when Maria said the name it sounded like *on* "—how nice you can come." When she pulled me against her, holding her arms around my waist so tightly that I felt all her body against mine from chest to knees, she lowered her voice to husky provocative intimacy, whispering. "Martin"—*Maar . . . teen*—"my love. I am glad." She did not look behind me for Sally, and when I made a quick explanation of Sally's absence, Maria waved it away: it was clear that for her Sally's absence was not a thing of great moment.

We were the last guests to arrive. The others already sat around the room, glasses in hand, talking: Danzig, the Polish novelist, his wife, Helga, Maria's sister, Ursula, and an elderly white-haired American lady named Cartwright. Marek served drinks almost before we were seated, and when he came to pouring the chilled vodka for me, his face dared me to say "when" sooner than he thought properly manly and befitting the occasion. I don't enjoy drinking much. I don't like the taste of alcohol and I don't like the way it depresses me. People generally take that to mean that I get drunk easily, and nothing could be further from the truth. Perhaps it was because I had plenty of body weight to absorb the alcohol, perhaps because I didn't like drinking and had no intention of getting drunk, but whatever it was I didn't easily get pie-eyed. I had over the years tucked away as much and more than most men, though with the advancing years I had taken care not to drink on an empty stomach and even, before an evening of heavy drinking, to take the precaution of a tablespoon of mineral oil. All I want, an old friend of mine, now estranged, used to say, is a fair advantage; and that was all I took. But I never reached the point of enjoying it.

Drinking had always been a bone of contention between other people and me. Jews don't drink and are therefore less manly. Writers are supposed to drink; it invites the Muse. Look at Dylan or Scott or whomever. Publishers, editors and agents always softened you up for the negotiations or refusal to negotiate with the preliminary flatteries and martinis before the postprandial brandy-and-coffee realities. So I had also learned to drink to survive, learned to handle alcohol as part of the reality of American life in which I was immersed. Yet I had not forgotten the domiciliary virtues and puritanism of the wine blessed at meals which was a blessing to conviviality, but nothing more. Because of that there was often working in me the half-triumphant, half-bitter pleasure of watching those who had set out to get me drunk get drunk themselves, their eyes slowly glazing and going out of focus, their movements first becoming studied then uncontrolled, and finally their speech, that holy attri-

bute of the human, turning thick-tongued and bestial. With Marek
and Leszek, an evening could not be enjoyed without the protec-
tion? stimulation? lubrication? of alcohol, and when Anne and I
were there, or when Sally joined us, there was that eyelinked understanding of those on the sidelines who did not dance the polka.

Marek handed me a glass so full of vodka that I had to sip it
quickly to keep it from spilling over; and I had to keep myself from
knocking it back in a single draught as a gesture of bravado. I sat
and listened uncomprehendingly to the rattle of Polish talk around
me and thought how much the Torczyn house had changed. Maria
and Marek had given it an almost European air that was a triumph,
or at least a Parthian victory, over its Cape Cod, mass-produced
boxiness. Besides the money spent, the house showed the signs of
Maria's torrential energies and talents, and of Marek's taste and
travels. And Maria *was* a torrent, a female geyser of energy and feeling, a marvelous housekeeper, a superlative European-style cook, a
gardener whose thumb was so green that in the short space of a decade it had made her roses prizewinners at the local flower shows.

Everywhere there were traces of Marek's scientific peregrina-
tions, the conventions that scientists now went to as casually as
weekends in Atlantic City. A three-stringed *gusla* from Yugoslavia
hung diagonally on one wall; a serpentine chunk of California drift-
wood made into a lamp sat on a small Louis Seize end table; a magnificent Caribbean conch shell lay open and clamoring on the cock-
tail table. A semi-abstract painting in the early style of Kandinsky
showed two women in shifts, their backs turned and their heels dug
into Kentucky bluegrass as high as their thighs. They tried to hold
back two leaping, dark-red Irish setters. Right next to the painting
was an ancient cloth-of-gold tapestry with a woven battle motif ar-
raying a Polish peasant on foot in battle against a Teutonic knight in
armor on horseback. The Torczyn house held too many old things
for the straight lines of the architecture: it gave me an uneasy sense
of tension and misgiving that I could never quite master, as if I were
being called upon by an act of imaginative will to join unbridgeable
opposites, traditions that met, if anywhere, asymptotic to infinity.

Anne's eye caught mine, her face shaping the expression of sedi-
tious rebuke which every married writer knows as the disapproval of

his wife's soul; it does *not* say stop looking, or stop listening, or stop paying attention: instead, it commands, cajoles, cries out, "Stop observing! Stop eavesdropping! Stop gathering material!" In short, stop being a writer. As much use as to say stop breathing. Once Sally's sister, when she thought she saw herself in a story I had written, had burst out, "Martin's a sponge, a lousy old sponge soaking up people's feelings and thoughts, trying to soak up their secret lives, so he can squeeze them out into his writing." She hadn't meant that as a compliment either; and Sally had taken great care to convey her sister's tone to me when she relayed the comment.

The dinner did Maria and us proud. Spanish melon and prosciutto, *boeuf bourguignon,* saffroned rice, a huge escarole salad with chickpeas, and hot French garlic bread. Dessert was pear and boursin and port salut. All of it washed down with bottle after bottle of Valpolicella which Marek kept urging on everyone—no glass was ever more than half-empty before he refilled it to the brim. I enjoyed the food and wine and, seated as I was between Maria and her sister Ursula, both of whom did the serving, I was pretty much left out of the dinner conversation, though I listened.

Danzig, in slow, precise English, halting now and then to lapse into a Polish phrase which either Marek or Leszek translated almost without pause, told how he and his wife were going to see America, the *real* America, via Greyhound bus, making a great six-week loop through the country—Washington, D.C., New Orleans, the Southwest, Los Angeles, and San Francisco, then back through the Middle Western "heartland" to Chicago and finally back to New York. Leszek rebuked him for not including New England on the itinerary. Although it had taken Leszek some twenty years of living in the States before getting to see New England, he told the Danzigs that New England was the real heart and mind of America, its source and conscience, the fulcrum of political power, and should, therefore, not be bypassed. I had, over the years, heard many such conversations and they always left me distressed. Listening to Leszek and many other foreigners, visitors and those who had lived in the country for many years, I wondered if I had learned anything about the countries I had traveled in and the several I had lived in other than my own, for foreigners seemed to me always to have missed the shape, the essence, the meaning of America and its spirit. Yet, when I despaired that the country would forever elude them, I remembered de Tocqueville and Bryce: it was at least possible, even for intellectuals, to penetrate to the heart, though I knew that the America those two had analyzed was a far simpler place than America was now. And in the quiet of the nights, when I thought about it, I wondered if anyone, even those American born and bred, had penetrated to the heart of the country.

Danzig's face was interesting, strong, regular features, intelligent, reluctant brown eyes, and an almost effeminately mobile mouth. He wore the conventional European writer's uniform: gray tweed jacket with black leather elbow patches, dark gray trousers, a black slipover and dark tie which contrasted with a soft-collared white shirt. Much later, when we left, I saw that he even had the rest of the uniform, the double-breasted tan trenchcoat, epaulets and all, à la Camus or Humphrey Bogart, as you chose. Of course, he went bareheaded, though whether a navy beret was hidden in a capacious pocket I didn't know. The dark clothing gave Danzig a funereal air belied by the studied cheerfulness of his manner. He had the writer's watchfulness, of others and himself, but with Danzig it seemed the true writer's self-absorption: this was a man who lived with his finger forever on his own pulse. His wife, big, blonde, and Brunhilde-like, with a thick, beer-barrel strength that contrasted with Danzig's sapling slenderness, was altogether another sort, outgoing and really gay, with the air of having so often seen and endured—perhaps even staved off—the very worst that nothing and no one could frighten her again. Danzig looked a dapper forty-five, his wife an unkempt decade older, but perhaps that was because she watched him with a maternal alertness simultaneously touching and nauseating. Helga spoke no English though she said she understood quite well; but she would occasionally address me in schoolgirl French that indicated she understood considerably less than she thought—in both languages.

It was Maria's sister Ursula I watched most attentively. If the loss of one's mother tongue wrought havoc with a writer, as it had even with Leszek, who, in anguished transcendence that reminded me of

Conrad's epic wrestling with the language, had learned to write English with a purity of style imbued with a bleak Polish-Russian poignance that, at the white heat of his inspiration, managed to fuse all three cultures, for an actress the loss of her native language was catastrophic. Leszek had come first to England and then to America as a youth in his twenties; Ursula had arrived in the United States when she was more than fifty, bereft of any way to practice her art. Acting required companies, players, stages, most of all an audience that spoke the same language and shared the same traditions; of this there was none in the United States for a Polish actress, however talented and skilled.

Maria and Marek had brought Ursula to the States from Poland the year before and, with characteristic generosity, supplied affidavits and passage money for her and for her twenty-year-old daughter, Wiktoria, and then took the new arrivals into their house until they could find their footing. Wiktoria had picked up the language quickly, taken a job, made some friends—she was young, winsome, and pretty—and was already expert at the frug and the monkey; but for Ursula things were more difficult. She read English fluently and spoke it in a careful, grammatical way; but it was not enough to find anything but the simplest of jobs at a firm where she had to stand all day on a line packaging cosmetics. She and Wiktoria did not want to be burdens, not even dependents, so they took what jobs they could get because they needed the money. I had later tried to find Ursula a job on a Polish-language radio station, then on a small Polish-language newspaper, but I'd failed at both. Though I saw that she had lost weight she could ill afford to lose, that her face had grown drawn and paler, and that she was terribly lonely, I never heard her complain. Staying with the Torczyns saved her from the worst isolation and deprivation of new immigrants, but it also impeded her, kept her from being forced to make new friends and to rely on English for communication.

I liked Ursula, respected her courage and dignity, and enjoyed seeing her. It was not merely that she had once been an exceptionally pretty woman, that she was still lovely, with a strange, birdlike quality, as if she might suddenly take flight, but for the fact that one of her wings was broken. She bore a remarkable resemblance to the

Italian moving-picture star Guiletta Massina, but a combination of
the peasant girl Gelsomina of *La Strada* and the haute-bourgeoise
lady of *Juliet of the Spirits*. Married to Matthias Maciek, one of
Poland's foremost moving-picture directors and one of Danzig's
oldest friends, Ursula had led a stormy life with him for more than
twenty-five years until, four years before she left Poland, he had
divorced her for a twenty-three-year-old actress who was then his
leading lady. Maria had told me that this was the step which finally
persuaded Ursula to consider emigrating. Before that she had insisted that if Poland was for her a prison, she would not deprive
Wiktoria of a father so long as Maciek kept coming home—even as
infrequently as he did. The divorce was the watershed: after that,
since Maciek apparently felt only the most sporadic and brief desire
to see his daughter, Ursula saw no further reason for remaining in
the Warsaw *cul de sac* and she agreed to Maria's prompting to come
to the new world.

Brandy and coffee were served in a small sitting room that ad-
joined the living room; it faced out on a garden and through the
floor-to-ceiling thermopane windows I saw the Torczyns' bronze-
leafed plum tree, its brown-barked arms raised as if to pirouette.
Slightly stupefied by the flood of food, liquor, and conversation, I
sat silent until Leszek commented that I was unduly quiet and
Marek, pouring another dollop of cognac into my glass, said that I
was drunk. When that failed to produce the appropriate rise out of
me, Marek invited me to see some guns he had bought.

Marek's study was on the first floor of the house, a book-lined
room I knew well, for I had visited it often enough when Marek's
back had gone out of kilter shortly after Ursula and Wiktoria had
arrived from Poland to stay with them. I remembered particularly a
sweltering August day when I had come to bring Marek some books
and help him pass the time. Naked, except for white undershorts,
he lay there like an Indian fakir flat out on a board, hoping his disc
would slip back into proper alignment, his big frame gaunt, his face
pinched with pain, the skin over his bones an oil film that looked as
if it might evaporate if a breeze stirred. Before I could ask how he
felt, he had burst out: "It's a goddam harem, Martin! A harem, do

you hear? Five women in this house, and now"—a piercing groan—
"my mother's coming to visit too!"

I made jokes about sultans and harems and some men having all
the luck, but he didn't even grin; and then, for the first time, I noticed that his sideburns had gone completely white. It had been a
bad time all around and only after surgery and a back brace had
Marek been able to resume his daily round; by then he was a different man.

"How do you like these?" he asked, pointing to where an ancient
musket, a flintlock fowling piece, and a ball pistol hung on the wall.
I took each one down, as I was intended to, sighted down the bar-
rels, cocked them and went through the whole self-conscious
routine of appreciation while Marek told me about this little London greengrocer who had been inveigled into buying a truckload of
such antique weapons and had been unable to sell them. As a result
Marek had been able to buy those three beautiful old guns for a
song. Yes, *for a song*—his very words. I didn't ask what song they
were designed to sing, because I knew, a threnody that all of us in
the twentieth century knew well enough.

Abruptly, without transition, or so it seemed to me, Marek was
telling me about his father. On several occasions over the years I had
met Marek's mother, an old whitehaired woman, broad-boned but
thin, with an erect carriage and a face whose flesh had been win-
nowed away to the fine stubborn bones. Always in black, with little
white lace ruffs at the throat that called attention to the wrinkled
flesh rather than hiding it, she had the manner of a woman once
beautiful and still proud. Marek had inherited both her good looks
and her pride, and he sometimes talked of her, much less frequently
of his sister, whose picture sat on his desk and on the mantelpiece in
the living room, forever young, she having been killed in the Warsaw Uprising, but this was the first time he had talked about his
father to me.

Toying with the chased silver decorations of the ancient pistol,
Marek exclaimed, "*Absolutely without fear!* He was that kind of
man. A mad man." Marek looked up from the pistol. "Once we
went to the movies in one of the tougher sections of Warsaw. I
couldn't have been more than twelve then. We were sitting in the

theater, my father, my mother, and I, when someone behind us began to heckle my father about taking his hat off. And when my father ignored the heckling, the man began to make some abusive comments about that—toff?—'' Marek looked at me inquiringly, and when I nodded, went on, ''—not taking his goddam headgear off. My father stood up, turned around, calm and slow as you please, and gave the man a whack across the head with his walking stick, a heavy shaft of old walnut he always carried—and a riot started. I thought we were going to be lynched. The lights went on, the whole audience piled out into the street to get this toff, but my father simply led us out behind him, shielding us with his cloak and brandishing that stick, ready to do battle with all of them.''

''Without taking his hat off?''

Marek nodded, grinning. ''Without even considering it.'' He laughed. ''Mad. Absolutely lunatic. I guess *they* thought he was crazy too. They couldn't believe that he meant it. What man in his right mind takes on a whole neighborhood—the man he had coshed had dozens of friends there in the audience—and so calmly? So they let him march my mother and me through the whole damn mob of them though my father had opened that man's scalp from his crown to his ear and his friends were clamoring for our blood.''

''If you read enough books like *The Scarlet Pimpernel* when you're young,'' I remarked, ''you begin to believe that's the way a man must behave.''

Marek hesitated. ''Is that bad?'' he asked, but clearly he was not inquiring of me.

''Sometimes,'' I replied anyway.

Marek pulled the trigger of the pistol and the hammer clicked futilely. ''Yet, if they had asked him politely, with the proper *Pan,* I'm sure he would have removed his hat without a murmur.'' He replaced the pistol on the wall hooks. ''A gentleman's code.'' An uneasy silence fell, airless, between us.

''What happened to him?'' I asked, sensing his unspoken urgent desire to tell me about his father as if it were another presence in the room, a Banquo's ghost or *Doppelgänger*. To ask was very difficult for me: I had my own reluctance to ask Europeans of our generation that kind of question, especially Eastern Europeans.

"The Germans killed him," he said, slowly, taking a breath between each word. I had learned that expression well and long ago, not merely from having been in the war. It told of some brooks too broad for leaping. Ask an American such a question about relatives killed, even an American Jew, and he would usually say, "The *Nazis* killed him, or her, or them." But ask a European and invariably you hear instead, "The Germans," usually with a bitterly scatological adjective preceding. It said a great deal about their foreign policies and ours—and their histories.

I nodded. Recognition? Sympathy? Acquiescence? Sorrow? Shared injury? All of my father's family had perished. I never knew what that nod meant when I made it, but I knew that it hurt my stiff-necked human pride to be forced to it.

"My father was one of the Poles," Marek continued, "who knew it was coming back in '36 and '37. He wasn't one of the ostriches. He didn't think Poland was a great power, the way the Colonels did. So he tried to persuade some of his richer friends to set up a military hospital. He got all kinds of contributions, wheedling, cajoling, God knows how! He even managed to get one of his counts to lend him a castle! Then he started to put a military hospital together inside it. All by himself. By the time the Germans came in '39, beds, staff, surgery, almost all of it was ready, but they were desperately short of drugs. My father kept the hospital in medical supplies, scrounging things everywhere. Then one day he heard of someone on the outskirts of the city who was supposed to have a stock of morphine, a pharmacist, and off he went in the car to get it. By himself, of course. No one could be spared from the hospital, the wounded were flooding in, and he wouldn't listen to anyone's advice to take someone along with him, even a driver."

"And?"

"We found him three days later, in the car, dead. Germans were already in the suburbs. It was a German bullet that killed him, but it might have been one of our own *Volksdeutsch*. Nobody knew. No witnesses. Or at least none that we could find."

"All that courage coming to that," I lamented, and not for the elder Torczyn alone.

"Everything comes to that," Marek said. He carefully realigned the guns on the wall. "Absolutely fearless man," he repeated.

"An epithet? Or a compliment?"

"Always both for me, Martin. More epithet than compliment, I suppose."

"How Jewish that sounds!" I said, trying to make a joke of it.

Marek smiled, took my arm and led me toward the landing. "My mother is always hinting darkly, and privately, that way back there somewhere there's some Jewish blood."

"Welcome to another persecuted elite!"

"Don't I have enough trouble being a Pole?" he retorted, and the sentence had a singularly American ring.

Downstairs, Stanislaw Danzig and Leszek were deep in a quarrel about the hopelessness of contemporary Polish life. Leszek was scathing on the monopoly of all aspects of life by the Party and the dreary fact that the alternative was the medievalism of the Church, the Cardinal, and Our Lady of Czestochowa. Where, Leszek grumbled, could any man of good will, modern spirit, and clear intelligence find a place in contemporary Polish life? No wonder Polish young people were disenchanted, interested only in outlandish clothing, hairdos, and the wild irresponsibilities of rock-and-roll music and dancing when even the best of their elders had all been compromised by hypocrisy and cowardice, poisoned by gloom and lethargy and despair. As we sat down I caught Maria's raised eyebrow, but since Marek ignored it, I felt free to do so too: if explanations were forthcoming, they ought to come from him.

Sitting on the edge of his chair, Danzig patiently explained that geography was Poland's tragedy; forever caught in the nutcracker between Prussians and Russians, what else could Poland do? I saw that he was uncomfortable both because of the obvious political reasons—he was a guest from a Communist country, which required twofold discretions—and because of the necessarily careful choice of English words. But for Anne, Mrs. Cartwright, and me, and his own sensitive courtesy, Danzig would gratefully have lapsed into Polish. With a smile that was only slightly patronizing Danzig reminded Leszek that Leszek had been out of the country since 1940 and didn't know anything about the nation's postwar life, couldn't, in fact, understand it because he hadn't been obliged to endure it. In short, though Leszek was a Pole by birth and sensibility, he had forfeited his birthright by emigration, was now more American than European, more outlander than native, and could not therefore speak with authority and insight of the Polish predicament.

A few years earlier, when the dangers of arrest or imprisonment for emigres had for a time dissolved in the first lukewarm East-West rapprochement, Leszek had visited Poland to attend an international P.E.N. Club congress of translators. It had been his first trip since he had left the country with the Germans on his heels—and he had stayed for a month, traveling over most of the country. Until then he had sung the virtues of his homeland to us, romantically remembering Poland as superior to the crass refrigerator and corporation civilization of the States, proudly extolling Polish courage and gaiety in the face of adversity. No wry comments of mine about Colonel Beck or Marshal Smigly-Rydz, no minor recollections of their alliance with Hitler and the Third Reich until they were themselves threatened, no realistic notice of Polish living standards or political authoritarianism had been able to dispel his roseate vision. But the reality of Poland had. After his visit Leszek was bitterly disillusioned, critical of what he called "Polish reality" in ways which made even my crabbed comments seem generous and compassionate. "Truth," Leszek had said then, tears in his eyes, "they don't even recognize it any more. They don't know what the word means. My countrymen live under the lie, with the lie, for the lie. And they've lived that way for so long, tangled up with it like men entwined with a filthy whore, limb locked with limb, that they can't tell prostitute from wife any more." It was, for Leszek, an unsual image because, however inconsistently, he was extraordinarily prim and puritanical in his language and in his notions of what was acceptable sexual behavior.

I reminded him of observations Orwell and Aldous Huxley had made decades ago, and of his own Polish Czeslaw Milosz's more recent notion of "controlled schizophrenia," particularly among Polish intellectuals and Party members. What they wrote, Leszek fulminated, was nonsense. All the Poles were simply cowards and liars, and flattered themselves by thinking that they were being political realists, detached and objective, when they were in fact barely able to keep their proverbial stuck-up noses out of the ruck of the big lie in which they were immersed. Where they were not knaves and Soviet sycophants, Party hacks and fools, they were naive and ignorant of the world as it was. Now, pointing his finger at Danzig like a prosecuting attorney at a trial, Leszek insisted that Poles no longer knew the truth, about their own or the outside world, because even those who were in so-called opposition had swallowed so much of the Party line they didn't know fact from fiction. "And that's why we have no literature, no novels, no stories, no poems, no plays, that speak for Poland," Leszek concluded. "Even the Russian writers and intellectuals have more courage."

"Yes," I murmured, hoping to smooth things over, yet maintain the truth, "but so recently and so discreetly." No one seemed to have heard me. "And much of that ugliness comes not simply from cowardice or venality, but from being locked up there for two decades for Poland and more than four decades for the Russians. Having people like Mr. Danzig travel, letting him see the world with his own eyes, his own way, may help matters."

A slow flush rose up from Danzig's collar to his temples. He drew back in his chair, as if to hide in its recesses. "You cannot understand what it is like," he protested to Leszek.

"I saw. I was there. Warsaw. Cracow. Lublin, Gdansk. All alike," Leszek insisted, his hand chopping the air with each name like a guillotine. "Cut off! Provincial! Sunk in the muck and mire of pieties: Catholic, Marxist, nationalist."

"You cannot know," Danzig repeated, his mouth trembling, his head sad and shaking.

Marek tried to intervene then, to dissipate the heat of the argument, remarking that Polish writing was the best in Eastern Europe, and so were Polish films, paintings and sculpture. How much could one expect under the circumstances?

"Under the circumstances!" Leszek roared, incensed. "That pernicious phrase! The rotten apple in the garden. My God! Under the circumstances! You make art *out* of the circumstances, *because of* and *in spite of* the circumstances, not under the circumstances. That's why none of you have done anything important. Because you

write *under* the circumstances. To hell with the circumstances!'' He, for one, Leszek insisted, refused to demean Poland by comparing its achievements with those of its ''Balkan'' and ''barbaric'' neighbors. If Polish accomplishments could not be measured against France's, Russia's, England's, America's, yes, even Germany's, then the hell with it.

To divert the ferocity of Leszek's attack on Danzig, I tried to give—to impose?—some detachment and historical perspective on the discussion and in so doing, of course, made an error and committed a rudeness far more profound than Leszek's fierce concern. I said that writing under the circumstances, precisely because of what Danzig called Poland's tragic geography, had always been the tradition of Polish arts and letters, that as a result Polish writers and painters had always suffered from provincialism, from being cut off from the rest of Europe not only by their political misfortunes, their continual partition among more powerful neighbors, but by its nationalist consequences, so that even the heroic Mickiewicz had not been able to transcend that provincialism, not been able to rise above the boundaries of his language and culture.

Poetry, Danzig almost spat, is what is left after a work of art is translated from one language to another. I knew the line; however unwittingly, I had struck him, I saw, a far more grievous blow than Leszek had. And I was *not* a Pole and consequently *not* forgiven. In a slow, bleak chant, Danzig keened his lament that only that literature lasted which was attached to and disseminated by great political power. The literature of England had reached its peak in the sixteenth century when England became a great power. The age of Elizabeth I had produced Shakespeare and Marlowe and the greatest burst of literary genius Europe had ever known. When Louis XIV made France the leading power on the continent, Corneille, Racine, Molière, Pascal, La Fontaine, and Rochefoucauld were the natural consequence. The same was true of nineteenth-century Russia when, for the first time, the land of the Tsars became a power to be reckoned with in Europe; and it was also true of nineteenth-century America, first come to great power and to great literature after the Civil War. No, Danzig mourned, his words a dirge, it was not the quality of the writing, nor even the genius of the artists,

but the power of the guns, the network of foreign trade, the wealth
of the mines, the fields, the factories, and the banks that brought the
literature of a nation to the attention of the world and conferred
greatness upon it. Though I saw some truth to what he said, I also
saw no need at that point to put my finger on the flaw in his logic;
that is, to remind him that perhaps part of the thrust that brought a
nation to political and economic greatness was involved in bringing
its arts to flower as well.

Danzig had had his nose rubbed in it in America already; I did not
wish to add to his discomfiting. Leszek had taken Danzig to one of
the leading American magazines to see if it would publish his translations of some of Danzig's best work. The editor, a man of world-
wide reputation, had never heard of Stanislaw Danzig; and if he
hadn't, then Danzig and his work couldn't be of much importance.
His magazine, one of the redoubts of the so-called WASP Establish-
ment, would therefore *not* be interested in publishing Mr. Danzig.
The editor had spoken of Poles and Polish writing with that faintly
supercilious Anglophile snobbery which made Poland sound like
Outer Mongolia. Another editor, whose avant-garde magazine had
pretensions to an international, multilingual, and intellectual audience, had at least read two of Danzig's stories in French translations. But he said that no one in America gave a damn about Polish
writing and refused outright even to look at Danzig's manuscripts.
At the most illustrious Jewish literary magazine, Danzig, hopeful
that there at last he would find a sympathetic ear, was brimming
with stories of what it had been like to be a Jew and a writer in
Poland during the long nightmare from 1939 to 1945, but the editor,
bored and indifferent, had not even asked to look at any of Danzig's
work.

Because of these findings, and though I had not intended it, I had
struck Danzig a painful blow where he lived: I had said that his own
work, that painful distillation of his time and place, his feeling and
experience, had no pertinence outside of Poland; I had privately
confirmed and sealed his public rejection. Now I was aware of what
had happened, but the damage was done. Worse, I genuinely believed in what I said and in the logic of my position—that snare and
delusion of intellectuals!—though it moved against the grain of my

feeling and consideration for Danzig the man; it had carried me beyond the bounds of courtesy. I reminded Danzig that some writers did translate, did transcend time and place and language, that one could read Sophocles or Job or Dante with pleasure and pertinence without being able to read ancient Greek or Aramaic or medieval Italian; this was not true of Mickiewicz, for example, whom I had read in several English translations, verse and prose.

"The translations are all terrible," Leszek interjected. "Worse than terrible, banal."

Moreover, I added, the Bible, for one, had been written by a people without much political or economic power. In fact, the Israelites were nowhere as powerful as the empires among which they had lived and with whom they had contended—Egypt, Persia, Babylon, Rome—but their literature had outlived that of all those great kingdoms. It had even almost transcended the language of its original, being read and enjoyed and cherished in Latin, Greek, and English, among many other languages, while only a tiny remnant still read the ancient Hebrew. The great empire, the true kingdom, I concluded sententiously, is of the spirit.

"Mickiewicz," Danzig said, so slowly he seemed to be gasping for air, "is a Goethe, a Shakespeare, an Isaiah—yes, *our* Goethe, *our* Shakespeare, *our* Isaiah. More, one cannot ask."

For an instant the Delacroix drawing of Mickiewicz stood before my eyes, the long hair, the aquiline nose and strong jaw, the heavy-lidded eyes and sensual mouth: it was almost as if I were in the act of insulting the man as well as the poet. "No, Mr. Danzig," I said, "the mournful truth is that for the great geniuses, for the great works of art, the truth of the human heart, not the truth of the nation or the state, is the essential truth, perhaps the only truth." To my astonishment, I saw that Leszek was nodding vigorously. "Because of that," I continued, "Sophocles and Dante are read everywhere, while Mickiewicz is read only in Poland; and because of that Dostoyevsky and Balzac will be read wherever men continue to think and feel, when Sienkiewicz and Reymont are only footnotes in the histories of European literature." I was sorry I'd been carried away and made a speech, carried away not only by my logic but by my rhetoric; and now I could have bitten my tongue.

"And the Bible," Danzig asked poisonously, "when the Jews have been forgotten?"

"That, too, I suppose," I answered, "because the single human voice speaks to the single human ear and heart over the centuries and the distances as nothing else does."

"Perhaps even the single human voice can't be heard now," Anne remarked, "perhaps it never could. Perhaps what survived survived only by accident, and what is considered great is great only by illusion." She spoke with her most sibylline expression, her pink tongue licking her dry lips where a fleck of cigarette paper was pasted, as if the words were too arid, too desertlike for her lips to speak unmoistened. Except for Mrs. Cartwright, whose bright, birdlike cheer remained unchanged, everyone turned grimly to Anne, hoping that her face would contradict with laughter, or even a grimace, the unrelieved aridity of her voice and words, but Anne's eyes were downcast, the eyelids dark, with the shadow of the future, or makeup.

Maria said too loudly that there was too much talk, too much brains, and called for more vodka and more dancing. She tuned the hi-fi up and ordered everyone to dance. The three married couples rose obediently, Ursula went to the kitchen, and I was left with Mrs. Cartwright. Politely, I asked how she was enjoying the party and in a high-pitched, Julie Andrews-like voice she told me she was having a marvelous time. It was so much more interesting than the usual parties she went to. Foreigners, she smiled to take the sting out of the word—I knew what she meant, didn't I—were just plain more fun than old Americans, weren't they? Her white, perfectly coiffured hair, her sparkling dentured smile and remote kindly brown eyes terrified me more than the black depths of Danzig's eyes or the bitter distances of Anne's: they were from another world altogether. She hadn't been to such a party for the longest time, she said. How good it was of the Torczyns to invite an old lady like her, a widow, to such a shindig. Yes, *shindig,* that was the word she used. How her husband, Malcolm, would have loved it! He'd been a lawyer, in real estate, you know, and he did so enjoy drinking and talking to people. I saw the tears start to her eyes and turned away, embarrassed, as much for myself as for her. Had she understood anything she'd heard that evening? Or had age and temperament simply removed her from the suffering and the struggle to the extent that the sound of human voices and the warm gurglings of digestion were enough to make the party perfect for her? Or did any party revive her feelings for a husband long dead and still mourned?

The records being played were fox-trots, waltzes, tangos, and rhumbas, all of which I danced well, but I surmised that as the evening wore on and the level of intoxication and despair rose, so would the tempo of the music quicken. Rock and roll would come soon enough, too soon for me; we could no more live in the terpsichorean past than in the historical. I asked Mrs. Cartwright to dance and as I held her at arm's length was not at all surprised to find that she smelled of lavender and danced a dainty, small-stepping fox-trot. In the next hour I danced in succession with Mrs. Cartwright, with Helga Danzig, Anne, Ursula, and Maria, and noted that each had her own particular style—and the style was the woman. Helga Danzig danced just the way she looked: big, clumsy, almost impossible to lead; dancing with her was like pushing a weight uphill, but the weight bore you no malice and was as good-natured about stepping on your toes as about your stepping on hers. She talked all the time we danced, telling me in her schoolgirl French how sorry she was that I had stumbled into such a discussion with "her Stash," because he was having such a bad time of it in the United States, the reality of the country having shocked into smithereens his preconceived notions of what America was like. Anne danced beautifully, with sinuous grace that was half-surrender, half-withdrawal, holding her body away from mine as if she understood and mistrusted its capacity to arouse, but wanting, crying out to be lifted off her feet, swept away. She danced with her eyes closed, permitting herself to be pervaded by the music and the movement, opening her eyes only when, as if by some inexplicable telepathic signal, she knew Leszek was heading for more vodka. And her eyes always opened at just the right time. Ursula danced as if she had no partner at all, belonged to no one and to no place, but was doomed to be the center of attraction for all eyes, yet a fey spirit never to be held in any single pair of arms. I did not dance with her so much as beside her, permitting her to express and display herself. Around her neck an old gold necklace with a strange modern pendant was hung; the pendant resembled a surrealist version of a crucifix and seemed both sacrilegious and appropriate as it whipped frenziedly against her breast, shoulders and back, as if she were being scourged, as if she were scourging herself, for dancing.

But for me Maria's dancing was the most disturbing. If Marek had been asked he would probably have said that he was one of the prime examples of the division of the two cultures—what Leszek called the great literary "snow job"—but he would have been excessively modest and perhaps talking about the wrong two cultures. Marek was an intelligent man, not quite an intellectual, for whatever good or evil that term portends, with an abiding interest in culture and politics. If he lacked Leszek's linguistic flare and poetic flame, he was nonetheless fluent in English, French, and German besides his native Polish and had, I knew, only two years before taught himself Russian simply to keep pace with what Soviet biologists were doing in his field. Maria was different. If asked, she would have insisted that Marek was not interested in literary things; but as far as I could see she loved the literary chiefly for the *vie bohème* she thought went with it, the excitement, the drinking, the sex, the gossip, the gay life she had once known after Warsaw in Paris, Madrid, and on the various seacoasts of France and Spain. It was a life she sorely missed, and the milieu was perhaps her natural element. If writers interested her, and they did, their books bored her; if the writer's life intrigued her, his work and his commitment to it exasperated her: she preferred parties to persistence, sex to creation.

And dancing with Maria was a sexual experience. She danced with her body as if by nature and art she should fit every curve of it into her partners' and so become part of them, make them a part of her. Insistently provocative, she was a landscape of desire, but difficult if not impossible to lead on the dance floor. Yet she was a graceful dancer. You saw when you watched her and felt when you danced with her that as a little girl Maria had gone to the right dancing masters, white gloves, dancing slippers of proper patent leather, frilly pink organdy dresses, and all; and there she learned the intricacies of the various dance steps as well as the regal posture that was so natural to her. The school had shaped her grace, framed it around a molten steel core that had little or nothing to do with it, and that core was neither graceful nor easily led. How she and Ursula could be sisters never ceased to astonish me, and now dancing with them one after the other made the bafflement as unbearable in a tactile and kinesthetic way as it had been before psychologically: where Ursula melted from the touch, Maria stood fast; where Maria threatened to prevail, Ursula seemed committed to doom.

While we danced Marek went around filling glasses and then stopped to talk to Danzig and Helga, who sat, hands entwined, next to each other on the couch. Leszek, quite drunk now, held Anne close to him, both hands on her shoulders, his eyes shut behind his glasses. They moved only slightly, in a slow, sensual two-step that fastened their bodies as close together as Maria had endeavored to fasten ours. "Look at them!" Maria exclaimed admiringly in my ear. As she spoke, Leszek opened his eyes, looked glassily down at Anne, and said loudly. "I love you, Anne." He noticed us then, saw us watching and listening, and proudly proclaimed, "You see, Martin, I love her. She's my honey." He hugged her to him in an embrace at once so Polish and unselfconscious that it was a joy to behold. Alcohol did have some salutary purposes for him. Anne, color on her pale cheeks, burrowed her nose into his shoulder, and they danced off.

Talking into my ear, Maria sent chills down my spine. "You know how is with Marek and me. I never want to marry with him. He wanted, never me. But he make me to marry. He write the papers, because we are in England and must have papers. The other way is all right with me. Because we don't have children, I don't care. You know the children is not mine, we are adopting." Her shallow intense breathing, her quivering rib cage emphasized what she was telling me, though I had known it long ago and she had, over the years, told me herself several times. She had also forgotten that she had told Sally, who reported it to me, that if she did not want to marry Marek, she wanted to have him, live with him; and she had done everything to keep their liaison alive—even, at the last, marrying him. "See how they are!" she gestured at Anne and

Leszek, still caught up in their slow, sensual music. "Is marvelous! A man have guts to say I love you. But must be able to say. Leszek has guts to say. Marek not . . . no guts."

For a few moments, the rhythm of the music and mood combined in a fugue of sympathy for Marek, knowing how difficult such demands, spoken or silent, were when made in a marriage and thinking, not without pain, of Sally. I knew Maria was wrong, that in such matters there were different courages and cowardices, as many as there were men and women, that diffidence was not always cowardice, that words were not always commitments nor silence the absence of feeling. It was not until I heard Maria say *Sally* that I realized she had continued to speak and was now talking about me. "You are disappointed man," she breathed into my ear, "and I know why you disappointed. You brilliant . . ." she sensed my reaction and reiterated " . . . yes, you brilliant man, but do not get what you expect, what you want in heart." I had not, she said, received the recognition of my talents as a writer, nor been given proper appreciation as a man; I had not managed to find what I wanted or merited in a woman. What Maria thought I wanted was a different woman from Sally, not one who sallied forth—the pun came to mind inevitable and unsummoned—to her laboratory and career, but one who remained at home and made me—*me!*—the center of her life. The responsibilities of a marriage in which I was the axis around which another human being's whole life rotated were stifling—and terrifying. I was a lover of more freedom, or at least of more tether—and too much of a coward to undertake such plunges into chaos. As my feet moved in the orderly fox-trot steps, they had to be kept from running away. I forced myself to listen and watched the play of feelings on Maria's face until gradually I saw that she thought she was talking about me and Sally but was simply, perhaps not so simply, talking about herself and Marek. With a sharp intake of breath, she said briskly, and in what seemed to me a non sequitur, "I love you, Maar . . . teen. You know this," as if that explained and summed up everything.

I love you. Was that Maria's usual hyperbole—I *love* pilaf and Hermes scarves and Maserati cars and benedictine and brandy—the exaggeration of language that vodka and her limited English vocabulary imposed on her tumultuous temperament? Or was it simply the echo of the Costa Brava and the Costa del Sol, the Rive Gauche and the Cote Basque, Tangiers and Como, Soho and Greenwich Village, the you're a writer and interesting, and most of all you aren't my husband, so tonight, here, now, I love you, because you are strange, spare, different—*in*different?—and what it means is that I want you to make love to me? Or had she truly understood what she'd remarked on in Anne and Leszek and felt that she had missed that? Before I could ask, or she could answer, the record ended; the dance was done.

Mrs. Cartwright stood up, ladylike and still perfectly groomed, not a white hair out of place, though the rest of us showed the late-hour dishevelments of drinking and dancing and arguing; and Maria, the perfect hostess, hurried out of my arms to her side. Mrs. Cartwright murmured how late it was for her, how wonderful the party had been but she was an old lady and couldn't keep her eyes open after midnight even, a moue and a dentured smile, for the late, late show; but her eyes sparkled like rusty wet bolts and she seemed livelier and wider awake than any of us except the indefatigable Maria. Everyone rose and went through the ritual of trying to persuade her to stay, but Mrs. Cartwright would not permit herself to be persuaded. As she titteringly allowed it, the assembled Polish males each in turn bowed and kissed her hand; and then, having dismissed her, went back to the serious business of drinking, dancing, singing, and quarreling while I accompanied Maria and Mrs. Cartwright to the door, not out of politeness but because I thought I might, before the moment passed entirely, get a word from Maria about what that *I love you* really meant. Only when we were in the vestibule helping Mrs. Cartwright into her coat did I realize that I was delighted we had been interrupted: I didn't really want to know. As I lifted the coat over her shoulder, Mrs. Cartwright turned her head to me, a quick coquettish swerve that smoothed the lines from her cheeks and throat, a gesture she had probably seen Vilma Banky perform for John Gilbert oh so long ago. "Your talk was so . . . stimulating, Mr. Wallace, so . . .exciting! How Malcolm would have enjoyed it!" Her eyes clouded with tears and her lips trembled. "To be killed playing polo! How simply stupid!" she grated, then gave my hand a fleeting kid-glove squeeze and swirled out of the door.

While Maria closed the door I asked how long Malcolm Cartwright had been dead. "Is sixteen, seventeen years, maybe," she replied, abruptly cold and brusque. "Right after war."

"Did he really die playing polo?" I asked. Was that so unreal? so remote as I found it? And was Mrs. Cartwright herself?

Marie shrugged. "Maybe. Does not matter. He is dead."

Leszek stood in the classic posture of the orator, one hand pressing his vodka glass to his heart, the other arm outstretched, index finger pointing to the distance beyond the thermopane doors where the bronze tree outside elegantly raised its arms. As I sank down on the couch next to Anne I asked her softly what he was reciting. She had studied Russian and had, after all, lived with Leszek and his emigré Poles for half a dozen years. "Don't understand a bit of it, thank you," she said. "And I don't want to learn."

Marek, standing next to us, overheard. "Makes your life a bit more peaceful, eh?" he inquired. "You can turn us Poles off."

"No, only sometimes and only some Poles," Anne replied.

"Leszek's reciting a Mickiewicz poem, 'At the Grace of the Countess Potocka,'" Marek explained. In deliberately singsong English, with baroque inflections, he translated:

> O Polish beauty I too die in exile:
> Let kind hands strew this earth on me then,
> And when wayfarers stop and speak of you,
> I shall rise from my sleep to hear our own precious tongue:
>
> Let him who sings your sorrows once more to life,
> Seeing my grave nearby, make my sorrows a part of his song.

Under her breath, in a reedy soprano, Anne mockingly sang, "And I'll rise with my trumpet from out of my grave our own glorious Emperor defending."

"*Your* grenadiers were traveling west, but defeated," Marek commented wryly.

"And these?" I asked.

"Stashu challenged Leszek's right to speak of Poles and the Polish way of life again," Marek said, "and Leszek is quoting Mickiewicz to give him the lie."

"Again?"

"Again," Anne interjected.

"Does Leszek really have to establish his *bona fides?*" I joked.

"With appropriate verses from Poland's epic poet?"

"His Polish honor is at stake," Marek said, straightfaced.

"When he's drunk it is, anyway," Anne amended.

Anne and I went to the kitchen and left the Polish, flying thick and fast, the voices loud and emotion-charged. There, at the kitchen table, Anne poured two cups of coffee from the electric percolator, and we sat. The coffee was hot and strong and I drank it in grateful silence. "I'm irretrievably middle-aged," Anne said, not looking at me. "They can go on like that all night, night after night, eating and drinking, dancing and singing, talking, arguing, discussing. After midnight, I've had it."

"Middle-aged? Not you, Anne, you look the same as when we first met."

"Ah, Martin, gallantry will get you everywhere."

"It's been a long time, hasn't it?" I asked.

Anne smiled. "A very long time, Martin."

"After eleven o'clock at night, there are only three things I want to do: sleep, read, or. . . ."

" . . . yes, I know," she interjected, laughing. "I know you."

"I mean it."

"I know you do."

"What civilized person is different?"

"Only those 'barbarous' Poles." Anne inclined her head toward the other room.

We laughed together.

I asked if Leszek actually meant to move to Maine.

"He'd like to. In one way I can't really blame him. It *is* a lot cheaper up there. We could live on half of what it takes here, and that would take some of the strain off him. He could do a lot more writing and a lot less of the translations he has to do for money."

"And you?"

"I don't have much family left. My mother and my sisters are here, and my younger sister's going to have another child in a couple of months. . . ."

" . . . Congratulations!"

"Always an aunt and never . . ." her voice trailed off.

And then, because the hour was late, because I had had a great deal to drink, and because I saw the falcon and sparrow halves of Anne's face in bitter conflict over the coffee cup, I asked if Leszek had changed his mind about having children.

She shook her head.

I told her I had talked to Leszek about it during the spring when he and I had gone to see an exhibit of modern Polish painting. I had remarked, altogether too casually of course, that I'd come to the conclusion, properly belated, that I had been foolish not to have children earlier and not to have more than two.

"Returning the compliment, Martin?" Anne asked. Years before, when Leszek was still married to his first wife and I was still adamant against bringing another Jewish child into the world after Auschwitz, Anne had pleaded with me not to be a fool. Sensibly and eloquently pleaded. It was a long time before I listened and then not until I was listening to myself far more than to her. I remembered and I knew that she remembered too.

"Maybe, but I talked because I really think he's wrong. Oh, I know why he's reluctant, maybe more than most anyone, but I think he should change his mind not only for your sake, but for his."

"Too late," she said, "altogether too late."

"You're not that old."

"No, but Leszek is."

I manufactured the leer I knew she expected and said, "I think he can make it."

She ignored me. "I don't even blame him, I suppose. Much as I'd like to. He's going to be fifty next year. And next year his son will be out of college, his last support payments finished at last. How can I ask him to start that whole thing all over again?"

"But *you* want a child?"

She nodded, dumbly.

"Then tell him so."

"Don't you think he knows?"

"Sure. Leszek's sensitive and perceptive, but he doesn't know how much."

"That's not something you communicate with words."

"You have other methods as well."

"Not with anything." There was iron in her voice. "If you have to, then it doesn't work, it won't help, it doesn't matter." She drank her coffee down to the dregs and made a face. "This is Leszek's last chance to write his own poetry, free of wars and imprisonment and alimony and child support. His last chance. I won't ask him to give it up."

"Yet *he* is asking you to give up having a child."

"My last chance too?" She smiled a self-deprecating grin. "Woman's role, you know. Sacrifice. Renunciation. Bowing the head."

"Borsht!"

"No, money."

"Is it only the money?"

"Only!" she exclaimed impatiently. "Don't be stupid, Martin. And don't play dumb either. You've lived through it. You know what it's like. Sure it's a matter of money, and strength, and time, and of not being so young any more, of not being able to start the whole damn cycle over again."

I thought she was going to cry, with anger and frustration, so I went around the table, put my hands on her shoulders, and was shaken off. Everyone, I thought, in politics as in marriage, buys his fulfillment with someone else's frustration; everyone buys his freedom with someone else's bondage. I left her alone there, as I knew she wanted to be left alone.

In the quiet of the upstairs bathroom, the voices below seemed the most distant muttering, like wind in the leaves, and I tried to put the same distance between me and the voices echoing in my head, but I couldn't. Not even the cold water on my face and wrists, or the wet comb through my thinning hair, helped; and the dash of Marek's shaving lotion on my face only made me aware of the stubble of my beard and left me unrefreshed. As I was about to go down the stairs,

Marek's and Maria's eight-year-old Irena came out of the bedroom
in a blue nightgown, her eyes closed, and groped her way into the
bathroom. When she emerged, one eye opened for a moment, she
stared at me and identified me. "Cover me," she commanded sleepily and then her eye closed and she stumbled back into the bedroom.
I followed, tucked her in, then rearranged the blankets to cover her
sister, Janina, in the next bed. For a long time I stood looking at
their small flowering faces, listening to their breathing like music.
All I could think of was how it would be for them when they grew
up, if we left them any kind of world to grow up in. Knowing that I
couldn't predict or probably even do anything about it, I turned on
my heel and went back downstairs.

The living room shook with the tuned-up sound of rock and roll,
the whine of electric guitars, the bleat of brass, the boom of drums
and cymbals: Chopin had gone and the world was too much with us,
late and soon. In the middle of the room, shaking to it, shaken by it,
her skirt hiked high on her slender thighs, Ursula danced to that
music, alone. Eyes closed, arms overhead surrendered her, arched
body gave her away, hips gyrating debased her; yet, with all its
naked desire and voluptuous longing, her dance was curiously
chaste, as if performed by a young girl before she was nubile, one of
those Balinese children whose sensually expert dancing betrayed
their innocence while mocking with their childhood the adults for
whom they danced. In another sense, too, Ursula danced as if she
were an old crone, past desire or fulfillment, who could still ape the
essence: Ursula's desire no longer expected or even required gratifi-
cation—there was no joy of man's desiring possible—it had turned
in on itself; whipped, it had curdled to a thickness of loving fear and
fearful love.

I don't know what the others felt as they watched—Leszek blinking nearsightedly behind his glasses, his face grim, his hands nervous; Anne's mouth tremulous and working, her face half-turned
away as if she couldn't bear to watch nor bear not to; Helga
Danzig's lips making silent words, frog-eyed—but no one moved to
stop Ursula. The music rocked and rolled and everyone, hypnotized
by the dance, the vodka, the fatigue, seemed old and beaten, like ancient savages squatting on the stony shores of some brackish lake in

the shadow of blackened Polish pines, watching their shaman dance for them, plead for them into the face of the indifferent gods. *Totentanz.* Why did the only expression that came to mind come in German? Frenzied, the Gelsomina of the night turned and twisted, leaped and cavorted, on her own road of pain, and on ours, the Pan I knew had not panned out and wouldn't.

Afterwards, still breathless, Ursula sat on the couch in the sitting room with me, her eyes metallic, her upper lip beaded with sweat. She gripped my hand and I felt the spasms that convulsed her body as if they were my own. The others by then were drinking fresh coffee Maria had prepared, yet Ursula stubbornly would only drink vodka, tumblerful after tumblerful, swallowing that deceptive ichor of fermented potatoes that promised exaltation but only pounded people into the dark of earth like the blind roots of tubers from which it came: the Polish curse and comfort. At my side, her trembling became words, grammatically perfect English delivered with limping caution that belied the headlong reckless timbre of her voice. "I am afraid to die," she said, gasping as if death were upon her. "Not of death, only to die. I cannot sleep. I cannot forget. I lie awake in the night, my flesh cold and wet, trembling that I will die."

All her life, she told me, had been a war, born in one, married and giving birth in another; even her marriage had been a war, to its death, yet in those days she never thought about dying. She had seen much death and many people die—Poland during the war was a veritable graveyard—but she was never afraid. Now suddenly she felt death near, like a garment she had left hanging in her closet and could not see or find though she knew it was there; the shroud in her wardrobe that would be her last cloak waited to envelop her and she could smell its stale fatal odor through the sachet and perfume with which she drenched her living clothes.

I tried humor, that weakest reed of the intelligence, and she looked at me perplexed. Her words and expression said—Ursula remained a skillful actress whose body communicated powerfully even without words—how can you be so unfeeling, how can your American insensitivity make a mockery of my naked terror? Her single sentence, "I am afraid to die," repeated now, was the sharpest rebuke. Ashamed, I told her that I was often forced to humor to guard my deepest feelings, that she was like all the rest of us in middle age: we had reached the stage where we knew death to be inevitable, knew ourselves not immune. If we had to live with that recognition constantly, if we were deprived of that magnificent and ignorant imperviousness of youth, it should—I almost said it must—make our lives more valuable, keener-edged to the touch, though I was not by any means sure that the conditional tense, that perpetual goad and tyranny of men and their language, could bear the weight of the logic any more than the reality could.

"And I shall die alone," Ursula said, as if she had not heard a single word of mine.

"You have Wiktoria," I reminded her.

"Not even divorce could take his claws out of me. Here." She let go of my hand and clutched her belly, her nails sibilant against the material of her dress. "I can still feel him . . . inside me." When she realized that what she had said was *double entendre*, her cheeks flamed and in a small voice she added, "And that only makes me more afraid."

Marriage, I thought, is a hand grenade with the pin out. You hold your breath waiting for the explosion. And when the grenade does, finally, go off, if it doesn't kill those close to it, it leaves them wounded or maimed and picking pieces of shrapnel from their flesh for the rest of their lives.

A story from my childhood came back and I told Ursula how the biblical King David, having been apprised that he would die on a certain day, had on that day barricaded himself against death in the room where the altar and holy Ark were kept. Gripping the horns of the altar in the traditional posture of pleading for mercy, David had thrown himself on the Lord's compassion and prayed all day for deliverance from death. But the Angel of Death was cunning. Late in the afternoon, he knocked at the door of the room and spoke to the king with the voice of his beloved Bathsheba. When the king opened the door to speak to her, the Angel of Death struck the great David dead.

"I understand him, your King David," Ursula agreed. She pointed across the floor into the living room where Maria, gesticulating with her coffee cup, was holding forth. "But her I do *not* understand. My sister. My *younger* sister. She believes. She is good Catholic, maybe not in primitive way some priests would like, but she believes in God. Even during war she believed. And she was not afraid to die then. She is not afraid now."

I wondered about how Maria drank and danced and fought and raised roses and wouldn't let any party end before dawn, and sometimes not even then, and I said, "We're all afraid, Ursula, all. Maria too."

Ursula reached for her vodka glass, found it empty, and lit another cigarette instead. "All. Yes. I know. But doesn't help."

"To know that everyone else is afraid too, that everyone else must die, sooner or later, and die alone?"

"No consolation. Nothing. So what must I do for consolation?" I gulped my vodka. "One must live. Every day. *Carpe diem.*"

Her laughter bordered on hysteria. "Americans! You are more old and cynical than all Europeans together. Even us Poles. And more naive." She began to sob. "One must live. Of course! Grasp?" she looked at me questioningly and I nodded her on, "the day. True! But how? Tell me that."

"I don't know that. I simply don't know."

Coughing smoke, the cigarette ash lengthening on her cigarette, she sat still except for her hand which crept back into mine and held it as if it were a life raft. The desperate always clutch at straws, I thought, with a bitterness and anger against myself I could not control or fathom. Abruptly she let go of me and, in one swift graceful motion that spilled sparks and ashes from her cigarette into her lap, removed her necklace and dropped it into my palm. "Here," she said, "I want you to have for Sally. Is from Poland. Has been in my family for long time. It is, I think you call an heirloom." She pronounced it *hair*-loom.

The pile of gold links and pendant were cold in my palm. "You know I can't take it."

"Is gift for Sally because I like her. Maria doesn't like. When I first meet I thought too she was cold woman, then I know she is shy. Like me. Not like Maria. Sally is very kind with me. I appreciate and would like to give necklace for my appreciation."

"I can't take it, Ursula."

"Because is gold? That does not matter."

"Not because it's gold but because it's been in your family for a long time, because it's part of home and home is far away."

"You must take." She folded her hands over mine and pressed the necklace into the flesh of my fingers until they hurt.

"Ah, you are making love with *my* Martin," Maria said, suddenly looming over us. "My big sister always takes the boys away."

"You look like you've done well enough in spite of that," I said.

"Maar . . . teen," Maria said seriously, "never can I tell when you are gallant or giving insult."

"Being gallant to you would be an insult, Maria," I replied. Then, holding out my fist, I opened my fingers to show the necklace. "Please, Maria," I pleaded, "ask Ursula to take this back."

Eyes flashed between the sisters, then Maria replied, "If Ursula give, she want you to have."

Ursula, her voice perfectly controlled, said she wanted to give Sally a memento of Poland and a token of appreciation—and that settled the matter. To protest further would have been to be a boor or an ingrate, so I made an awkward European bow and kissed Ursula's hand, though I vowed to myself that I would find some way to have Sally return that necklace without hurting Ursula's feelings, or without hurting them too much. By then Ursula would be sober and presumably more rational. As I came up from kissing that cold pale hand, its blue veins standing out like stigmata, the others were all grouped around us, laughing and joking at my European gesture, saying they would make a good Pole out of me yet, in spite of myself.

Anne finally prevailed on Maria to let us all go home. The party was over. We put on our overcoats and after a typically prolonged conference about who would drive whom home decided that I'd take them all to my house and Leszek's car there and then Leszek would take the Danzigs back into the city on their way back to Nyack. I'd take Ursula home. We walked across the Torczyn front lawn while Leszek, drunkenly, in a raucous whisper suggested we go back to the next-door-neighbor Poles and start the evening all over again. Anne, as if she had read my mind, whispered in my ear that that was why she didn't want Leszek to take Ursula home, though she knew it was out of the way for me to do so, but once he got off the parkways, they'd be lost for the rest of the night and most of the morning. Anne finally managed to maneuver Leszek into the front seat of the car while the Danzigs and Ursula got into the rear seat. I heard Maria call something and turned to see her and Marek framed together in the doorway, the light from behind them leaving them completely in silhouette. I asked Leszek what she had said.

"Why don't we go back and have one more for the road," he explained, and began to try to open the car door.

"Oh, God, no!" Anne said, and held him back. "Get in, Martin, and get us out of here."

We drove to my house in silence, except for Leszek's occasional "Now, honey . . ." spoken as if in reply to some rebuke of Anne's, but he never finished the sentence and she had never spoken a word to him. As he got out of my car to switch to his own, I asked if he would like to have some coffee at my place. Anne and Helga agreed but Leszek was adamant. "Just lead me to the parkway, Martin, I'll be fine."

"You're drunk, Leszek," I said harshly, "so why don't you have a couple of cups of coffee first."

"You remember last New Year's Eve?" he asked. "I was drunker, then, and I got home, didn't I? Tell him, honey," he appealed to Anne. When he saw that I was angry, he drew me aside, embraced me, kissing me on both cheeks as if he were a French general and I a *poilu* who had somehow survived the Marne and on whom he was bestowing a citation for valor. "Martin," he said in my ear, as if reading a decoration, "my friend, my good, my best American friend."

"Leszek," I responded, moved in spite of myself, "you reckless drunken idiot."

"No, Martin," he wagged his finger at me, "a saintly Dostoyevskian idiot. Alyosha. A divine fool. What can happen to me? I die? How many times have I risked that already?" He threw his arms out, widespread. "I owe a cock to Aesculapius."

We said goodnight. Danzig's handshake was a little gingerly when

I said I hoped we'd meet again, but tightened and grateful when I
told him, sincerely, how much I admired his writing. Anne's kiss
was a quick butterfly on my cheek, her hiss goodnight a caress in my
ear.

When I got back into my car, Ursula had already moved up to the
front seat and we were alone. I led Leszek and his car onto the
parkway, watching him in my rear mirror, and was relieved to see
his slow, too-careful, twenty-mile-an-hour pace until I had to turn
off, on Ursula's instructions. Only then was I aware that she was
crying, crying and smoking cigarettes, the lipsticked butts piled up
in the dashboard ashtray. I drove under an elevated with pillars and
old trolley tracks and cobblestones; to make matters worse hotrod
kids were coming home from their Saturday-night dates so I had to
concentrate on the driving. Besides, I could think of nothing comforting to say or do. Ursula moved closer to me, her shoulder
transmitting to me that same inner quavering that her hand had
earlier communicated, but when I made no response, she shrank
away and leaned against the door, as far from me as she could get.

I wished I'd been able to put my arm around her to solace her, but
that wasn't what she wanted or needed: and I couldn't provide what
she did need. I'd tried that more than once in my lifetime and I knew
how catastrophic it turned out: you didn't succeed in doing anything
but making matters worse, much worse; some things could not be
accomplished out of pity or compassion. Moreover, nobody rebuilt
anyone else's world; nobody could. Mostly nobody helped either—
without love and often enough not even with love. But surely not
with pity.

When I parked in front of her apartment house, Ursula asked me,
reluctantly, to take her upstairs because she was afraid to ride the
elevator alone. "You know I am afraid of so many things. Everything." She tried to smile but her eyes were frightened. I took her
into the lobby and we waited for the elevator. It was an old-
fashioned type with a grillwork door which had to be pushed shut
before it would rise. When I succeeded in slamming it closed, the
elevator began a slow, dignified ascent that would, in other circumstances, have been amusing. No sooner had it begun than Ursula once
more wept convulsively until I said, "Don't be afraid. It's only

a long sleep from which we don't wake up. That's it and that's all."

"It's not the death I am fearing," she sobbed, "it is the dying, the pain, the making myself dirty. Helpless. Feeble." She shuddered, gasping half-cries as if she were already stricken.

I grabbed her shoulder and shook her, gently, again and again, as if I were rocking a baby, until the cries died away and the elevator stopped at her floor. I took her key when her trembling hand could not find the lock with it, opened the door and held it open with my shoe while I gave her the key. "Is Wiktoria home?" I whispered.

Ursula nodded. "Thank you, Martin," she said huskily, speaking my name so shyly that I realized I'd never heard her use it before. It was as if we had just decided to call each other *du* or *tu*, or whatever the hell the intimate grammatical form for *you* was in Polish; as if we'd sworn a *Bruderschaft*—again a German word!—that was somehow a reassertion of our common humanity.

On the parkway dawn was coming up, a wintry red-streaked morning with black-and-blue clouds low on the horizon. I drove fast, breaking the speed limit without even checking my side or rear mirrors, and I kept the car windows wide open to let in the night wind, hoping it would blow the evening clear out of my brain—but it didn't. By the time I reached home, the sun was up, low over the houses, an apocalyptic ball of flame that threatened to consume everything it outlined with morning fire.

In the living room, I took off my coat and shoes, threw them on a chair and then, because my feet were cold, went upstairs to find my slippers. As I stooped to pick them up, I saw a slip of paper on the floor beneath them and picked it up instead. It was the torn-off half of a schoolboy's notebook page, and between the widely spaced blue lines, in my younger son's erratic printing, was red-crayoned, "You Martians get off our Planet. You are green. We are white. Surrender or we'll attack. Bang. Bang. You're dead and so am I." I stared at it for a long time until I saw the paper shaking in my hand. Then I took it into my son's room and put it back on his desk.

Downstairs, I poured another bourbon in the same glass I had left behind, what was it, twelve hours ago? and sank into my wing chair.

It was cold and I realized that I'd left the thermostat on the nighttime setting but I was too exhausted to get up and change that. Instead I took the afghan Sally always left on the couch and covered
myself. I must have fallen asleep then and what nightmares I dreamt
I don't remember, but in what seemed like minutes I was awakened
by the slamming of the front door. As I was about to get up, Sally
strode in and with one withering look surveyed me and the room.
"Look at you," she said disapprovingly, "just look at you! Sleeping in your clothes. In a chair." She bustled about, emptying ashtrays into the fireplace, picking up my glass and Anne's and
Leszek's ashtrays, refolding and replacing the afghan which had
fallen at my feet, all the while muttering under her breath.

"You weren't due back until Monday morning," I growled.

"It's already late Sunday afternoon," Sally said, her apology a
rebuke. I looked at my watch and out of the window, and plainly it
was. "I wanted you to have one good meal this weekend so I
thought I'd get back a little early and make us some Sunday
dinner." She was defensive and evasive at once. "Besides the boys
had some homework to do for tomorrow."

"Where are the boys?" I asked.

"Playing ball in the park with the Garrison kids," she replied.
"They'll be home in about an hour." She went into the kitchen and
I followed her.

"Well, how was the Torczyn party?" Sally asked over her shoulder, "or did you just stay home and get drunk?" She put on an
apron, lit the oven and began to take food from the refrigerator.

Stretching sleepily I wondered if I ought to be cross, and then
remembered Ursula's necklace in my pocket. I took it out and held it
from my fingers. "Here," I offered, "a gift for you."

Sally turned, instantly suspicious, and looked quizzically at the
gold links that glinted in the sunshine. "For me?" she asked.

"Yes. Maria's sister Ursula sent it."

"What in heaven's name for?"

For a painful moment I wanted to tell her, what in heaven and
hell's name for, but the moment passed with some deep breathing
and instead I reported, "She said you were kind to her, and she
wanted you to have a memento of her homeland."

"Poland?"

"Where else?" I replied noncommittally, but I knew it was the wrong answer.

Sally took the necklace and held it up in front of her, examining it closely. "It's gold," she remarked, "and probably an heirloom. Why would she give such a thing away? And to someone she doesn't even know very well?"

"She was drunk," I said shortly.

"Do you think I ought to keep it?" Sally asked, visibly upset.

"No. I think you ought to return it. With a kind note thanking her."

"Thanks, but no thanks, is that it?"

I stared at her for a long time to see if I had missed an irony, then I simply nodded.

Sally looked relieved. She paused and now it was her turn to peer carefully into my face and I, deliberately yawning and stretching sleepily, turned away. "I see," she said.

"What do you see now?" I asked sarcastically.

"I see that," her tone changed in mid-passage, "You'd better go up and get washed and shaved and let me get some dinner. The boys will be home soon and they'll be ravenous." She shooed me out of the kitchen and because there was nothing more that could profitably be said, or done, I went.